# A TIME

## and a

# PLACE

## SHORT STORIES

## Betsey Barber Hampton

**A TIME and a PLACE: Short Stories**

Cover art: Brad Stiller

Merlin-Janus Studio Inc.

Mooresville, NC

Publishing History

First Edition 2016

Print ISBN: 978-0692637623

Published in the United States of America

# A TIME and a PLACE

## Me and Charlie Brown

The big yellow sun was slipping out of sight when I heard the jingle of the chains on the singletrees as the mules and plows came down the driveway. I jumped off the porch, ran to meet Grandpa and Charlie Brown and asked if I could ride to the barn. Grandpa lifted me onto the back of the mule pulling his plow and walked ahead.

The mules sensed they had come through another long day of hard work slicing up the ground where cotton seeds would be planted. Soon they would be free of the bits that hurt their mouths every time the reins were pulled and somebody yelled gee or haw. The blinders and the harnesses would come off, then they could flop down in the barn yard, wallowing over and over on their backs, stretching their tired muscles and sore feet. They could taste the cool water in the watering trough and the sweet hay waiting for them in their stalls.

The barn was already in sight. They became anxious and quickened their pace.

The day had started as usual, with me waking up and finding Grandpa already up eating breakfast. I dressed and headed to the kitchen, where Cora was standing guard at the wood stove waiting to ask how I wanted my eggs. She was a large woman with a red bandana tied around her head. She wore an apron made from a flour sack and her big feet spilled over the sides of worn slippers.

A pot of grits bubbled on the back of the stove, a tray of fluffy brown biscuits was pulled to one side, and a platter of country ham sat on the table in front of Grandpa, who was blowing the coffee he had poured in his saucer, making it cool enough to drink.

I ate my fried egg, ham, and grits and smeared blackberry jam on a hot biscuit.

"I thought you were going to sleep all day," Grandpa said. "Me and Charlie Brown are going to plow the cotton field today. You help Grandma and do what she needs you to do, and we'll be in late this afternoon. Cora, fix Henry a plate. I'm going to call him to come eat."

Mr. Henry, who was too old to work, lived in a little house in our back yard. When he was a little boy, his stepmother kicked him out of the house, and he was taken in by a white family. Later, he came to live with my grandparents and was as completely devoted to them as they were to him. Mr. Henry was family.

My grandfather had a way of taking people in who needed a place to live. By the time he died, there were twenty people living in little tenant houses scattered around his farm. He was married at nineteen, made sixty cents a day with a baby on the way, so he understood hardship. He was the youngest of ten children. He used to laugh and say, "My mama told me if she'd known what to do, I wouldn't be here."

That day, after everyone had eaten, Cora put the leftover biscuits in a dark blue enamel pot that she kept in the sideboard in the dining room. Next to the pot was a jar of homemade pickles. I could treat myself to a biscuit and a pickle anytime my heart desired. Hanging above the sideboard was a picture of a basket filled with roses, one with a big bumble bee on it. They looked like Grandma's summer roses that grew pink and soft over the trellis on the front porch behind the swing.

Grandma always slept late, so I helped Cora clear the dishes and wipe the crumbs off the oil cloth on the kitchen table. I scraped the leftovers into a bucket that Mr. Henry would take to the pigs.

Beulah was in the back yard carrying water to fill the wash pot. She built a fire under it and came inside to gather up dirty clothes. "How you this morning?" she asked me as she got some lye soap from a shelf in the pantry.

While she waited for the water to boil, she sprinkled some shirts and dresses and wrapped them in a towel to iron after she finished washing. Once the water boiled, she put in the white things and added bluing. The smell of wood smoke and lye soap filled the crisp morning air. She stirred the clothes with a stick, then lifted them out and placed them in a tub of cold water before hanging them on a line to dry in the sun.

Beulah ironed on the screened back porch. The iron went thump, thump, thump as she ironed Grandma's blue dress. I played with my dolls at her feet and begged Beulah to let her daughter, Julie Ruth, come play with me.

I tried to impress her by singing a song my aunt taught me: "Oh, little playmate, come out and play with me, and bring your dollies three, climb up my apple tree, holler down my rain barrel, slide down my cellar door and we'll be jolly friends forever more. Oh, little playmate, I can't come play with you, my dollies have the flu, boo, hoo, hoo, hoo, hoo, hoo. Can't climb up your apple tree, can't holler down your rain barrel, can't slide down your cellar door, but we'll be jolly friends for ever more."

Beulah gave me a stern look and said, "Julie Ruth ain't gonna play with you. Her dollies ain't got no flu. She's got chores to do, and she know what happen to her if she don't do 'em. So you best go entertain yourself and don't be botherin' me."

By that time, Grandma was up and dressed. She ate breakfast and wandered about the house trying to find something to do. She got an oily dust mop and went over the floors down the hall and in the sitting room. She was kind of strange, like in a world of her own--- talking to herself and mumbling about all the bad things people did to her. She was always mad at somebody--- Grandpa, her kids, the neighbors or whoever she thought was talking about her.

I knew that wasn't quite right. She didn't pay much attention to me except when she wanted something, like her sewing box. Then she would say, "I'll give you a purty, if you'll go fetch my sewing box." I never saw a purty. I don't even know what one looks like.

Cora cooked supper and left it on the stove for us to eat that night. She had killed a chicken and fried it, boiled a pot of potatoes, fried a slab of fatback that she added to a pot of canned green beans, baked a chocolate pie, and made a pitcher of clear amber colored sweet tea. She swept and mopped the linoleum floor, set the table and finally went home to take care of her own family.

After Beulah finished ironing, she brought the clothes in from the line smelling like sun-warmed pine trees. Then she folded them before going home to see if Julie Ruth had done her chores.

So it turned out to be a long afternoon. Beulah had told me to entertain myself, and since Grandma was off in another world, I set about finding ways to do it. I went to Mr. Henry's house and found him sitting on his steps whittling. He gave me an extra knife and a piece of wood and showed me how to make a whistle. I whittled and listened to Mr. Henry saying, "Uh, huh" over and over again, until I got tired and looked for something else to do.

I walked to the grape arbor in the back yard and looked at the little green grapes forming on the vines. In a few weeks, they would be ripe, their juice ending up as a deep purple crystal jelly in little pint jars.

Beside the house was a fence of yellow jasmine that had just started to bloom, and in front of it was Grandpa's gold fish pond, covered with water lilies. Huge gold fish came to the surface, their little mouths popping up from underneath the lily pads, waiting for the pieces of bread I had brought. I never understood how they lived in that concrete hole and survived the winter, and nobody ever explained it to me.

Trying to entertain myself had made me hungry. I went inside and got a biscuit and a pickle before walking into the parlor, past the fireplace that still smelled of last winter's fire. Lifting the cover on the piano, I pretended to play as I watched the sun shine through the blue and gold glass beads that hung from the shade on grandma's lamp.

Then I wandered upstairs and walked around a great big room that held the three beds my uncles slept in when they were boys. A brick chimney ran from fireplaces in the downstairs sittin' room and bedroom up through the middle of the upstairs room and out the roof. The beds were still covered with the blankets that kept my uncles warm through the winter months.

Across the hall in my aunt's old room, I picked up her byelow baby doll, because I was still trying to find ways to entertain myself, like Beulah told me to do.

When I went back downstairs, Grandma was in the sittin room daring socks. I got a needle and thread out of her sewing box. She didn't notice me anymore than if I had been a fly flitting through the room.

I took the baby doll outside under the china berry tree and strung the white berries to make a necklace for me, and one for the doll. I had completely run out of things to do when I heard Grandpa, Charlie Brown, and the mules coming down the driveway.

I hurried out to meet them. Grandpa lifted me on the mule's back, and she started running. Suddenly I lost my grip, falling to the ground on my back, with one foot caught in the chains. Filled with terror, I realized the mule was dragging me towards the barn. It all happened so fast, I hardly had time to scream. But just as fast, Charlie Brown grabbed the reins, his big brown hands lifted me off the ground, and I was in his arms. I buried my face in his chest and cried my eyes out.

"You be all right?" he asked.

I guessed I was all right, but I wasn't the same person I'd been a few minutes ago, because at six years old, I had just learned the meaning of *grateful.*

After supper that night, the family went to the sittin' room. Grandpa loved to tell jokes and stories and he loved to laugh. His idea of fun was scaring me half to death. He told me about Jack the Giant Killer and a giant who said, "Fee- fi- fo- fum, I smell the blood of an Englishman. Be he alive or be he dead, I'll grind his bones to bake my bread."

I was terrified as I listened to the blood and gore tale Grandpa told me about Jack being up a beanstalk somewhere, because he was about to be thrown in an oven. And all the while, Grandma sat in her rocking chair. She was off in her own world, mumbling to *somebody*, but only she and God knew who that was.

Grandpa and I had this ritual thing we did every night before we went to bed. He would take me to the kitchen, get a big vegetable bowl, fill it with corn flakes, sprinkle a lot of sugar on top, pour sweet milk over it, get each of us a serving spoon, and we'd dig right in.

Then after Grandma went to sleep in her bed across the room from Grandpa's, I'd crawl in with Grandpa. He would turn out the light, and when it got real quiet, he would say, "Feefi-fo fum, I smell the blood of an Englishman. Be he alive or be he dead, I'll grind his bones to bake my bread!"

Well, that scared me wide awake! And then, to make matters worse, he'd scratch on the headboard and say, "Hear the mice? They're coming to bite you in the night!"

Even after Grandpa started snoring, I'd hear every tick and tock of the clock on the mantle as I lay waiting for the mice to creep under the covers and bite me.

In late summer, when the sun was blazing hot and not a breeze was stirring, the cotton field would be covered with a white blanket. It was waiting for the men and women who lived in the little shanties on the farm to come with burlap feed sacks strapped to their bodies and strip it clean.

They were in the field by sun up, and they picked until the sun set. Women brought babies and placed them on a quilt in a shady place, stopping from time to time to nurse them. They sang, "Swing low, sweet chariot, coming for to carry me home," as their aching backs trudged down row after row. They only stopped picking long enough to take a drink of water from a shared bucket and dipper.

One day Grandma made a cotton picking bag for me, from a cloth sugar sack. She placed a peach seed in the top corners to give it shape, wrapped a string around each seed, and attached a shoulder strap made from a piece of fabric. Some of the women in the field wore gloves with the fingers cut out to keep their hands from getting scratched on the cotton bolls, but I didn't get any gloves.

At the end of each day, we took the cotton to the barn to be weighed. If my little sack was full, it earned me a few pennies.

When enough cotton had been picked, it got loaded into a trailer hitched behind Grandpa's car, then taken to the cotton gin in Amity Hill. One afternoon, when the cotton was loaded and ready to go, Grandpa told me to hop into the car. Charlie Brown was leaning against the back rail of the trailer, which was old, dilapidated and open--- with only a few slats around the sides. I wanted to ride in the trailer with Charlie, instead. After all, he had saved my life. So Grandpa finally agreed.

Grandpa started driving across the field and up a hill, with the car bumping over the ruts. Suddenly the trailer came unhitched and started rolling backwards down the hill. It went faster and faster--- so fast I didn't have time to think. Charlie Brown grabbed me and held me tight, so I wouldn't be thrown out.
Finally the trailer came to a hard, jolting stop. It scared the living daylights out of me!

When Grandpa finally realized he had lost us, he came driving back. He laughed like it was all a big joke. Scaring me just made his day. I was getting an education--- sometimes more than I wanted. This was my second lesson in gratefulness.

At the gin, Grandpa waited in line for his turn to drive under the big pipe that sucked up the cotton, removed the seeds, then weighed and baled it. Next he would go into the office to get his money. He always gave me a nickel, so I could go next door to Christie's Store and buy an ice cream covered with chocolate and nuts, a "nutty buddy." Grandpa used part of his cotton money to buy chewing tobacco and smoking tobacco. It came in little cloth bags, with papers to roll it in. He kept his tobacco in a desk in the long dark hall that ran down the center of the house. The desk was made of apple wood, and the smell of tobacco blended in gave off a wonderful sweet and spicy aroma that filled your nostrils every time you walked by. The farm hands would knock on the back door when they needed tobacco, and Grandpa would see that they got what they wanted.

Those days represented a quiet, simple time. It was a hard time for many, but a good opportunity for a little girl to get a special education. My Grandfather taught me to be kind, respectful, and loving to everyone--- including my grandmother, who couldn't help being sick. And he taught me to laugh. I learned humility, compassion, empathy, and how to be grateful for all who provided love, care, and safety--- no matter the color of their skin.

Today they say *it takes a village.* In our village long ago, families were intertwined and every life mattered. Everyone made a difference in my life, but none quite like Charlie Brown. And one more thing---    I learned to entertain myself.

# Sundays at Aunt Lena's

Her house had its own personality and a distinct smell that was hard to describe, maybe a little like moth balls. If I was blind folded, I would know I was at Aunt Lena's.

That afternoon she answered the door bell in her little black polyester church dress with a fresh apron tied around her waist. She removed her white straw hat and laid it on the bed beside her black patent leather purse. The grandfather clock in the hall bonged 1:00. My family had driven into town from the country and arrived at the appointed time for Sunday dinner at my great Aunt Lena's.

But before we got to my aunt's, we went to church...

We listened to a long- winded, boring sermon, sang some old hymns out of a faded blue hymnal, and asked God to forgive our sins and guide us safely through another week.

I lived in the Bible belt.

My church was out in the country, an ancient brick, Greek revival building that sat back in a grove of oak trees. The long hard benches felt sticky from years of being coated with dark brown varnish. Red carpet, now almost threadbare, had been added down the aisles and across the pulpit floor. Any air conditioning we had blew in the open windows, along with the flies and whatever else God sent our way.

We sat on the left side of the church, next to a window that looked out on the green lawn and into the woods. I would have given my collection plate nickel to be in those woods. Silence fell on the congregation like a rock you couldn't lift when the preacher rose from his chair behind the pulpit and said:

"Turn in your hymnals to page 101. Please stand."

A rustling come over the room as we rose, stood straight and tall to sing:

*Onward Christian soldiers marching off to war, with the cross of Jesus going on before.*

Next came a long prayer, announcements of coming events, and a list of sick people who needed our prayers.

The preacher opened his Bible to Genesis chapter 6, verse 10, which basically said:

When Noah was six hundred years old, God decided He regretted making humans because they had disappointed Him. But since Noah was an honorable man, God would save Noah and his family, and drown the rest of the sorry lot in a flood.

Noah was instructed to make an ark out of gopher wood for his wife and three sons. He was also to save and a male and female of each animal that flew in the air or walked on the earth.

In the meantime, I wondered how so many animals could be crammed into an ark. Why didn't they kill and eat each other? What did Noah feed the lions, anyway? Likely there were a lot of dead bodies floating around, so maybe he got his sons to fish them out of the flood water and feed them to the lions?

I was looking out the church window at some squirrels jumping around in the trees and thinking there were probably mice and snakes out there, too. I wished God had just let those critters drown along with the sinners.

They were pretty much good for nothing.

A fly flew in the window and landed on my arm. Why was a pesky thing like that saved? I was fanning myself with a cardboard fan from a funeral home. The fan showed a picture of a handsome Jesus, with his long blonde hair curling around his shoulders. So I took the Jesus fan and shooed the fly back outside, thinking maybe it would go over to the pasture beyond the woods and land on a cow patty, where it would be a lot happier than on my arm. But I guessed being a fly wasn't too bad. It didn't have to worry about sin, because it was already saved, free to come and go as it pleased.

My mind flitted from the woods, where a woodpecker was hammering on a tree, to the preacher talking about six hundred year old Noah hammering on the gopher wood ark. He finished just before the heavens opened up, and it rained for forty days and forty nights.

I twisted and turned in the pew, smoothed my skirt over my legs before my mother pinched my arm and gave me her mean look that meant *be still or you'll get IT when you get home.*

The preacher's loud voice thundered through the church as he told us that if we displeased God we might not die in a flood, but we sure buddy would burn in hell. It got hotter and hotter in the church, and the pews got harder and harder. And I was thinking *this feels like hell anyway. I might go insane from the boredom of it all. I wouldn't be a bit surprised if the last judgment doesn't happen before we get out of here.*

The woman in front of me had a hat with pretty feathers that curled around the side. I wondered what kind of bird it had been. *If I was a bird, I would fly out this window over the trees and houses, somewhere where no one could find me. And I would just look down on the people rushing around and doing stuff, while I rested myself high up in a tree and let the wind ruffled my feathers.*

I had taken the pencil and card intended for visitors to fill out, and started drawing the woman's hat, when the preacher closed his Bible and opened the hymn book to page 330. We stood and sang, *"Amazing grace how sweet the sound that saved a wretch like me. I once was lost and now I'm found, was blind and now I see."*

There was another long prayer before the last and final amen, and then we made our way out to the entrance, where people stopped to tell the preacher what a wonderful sermon he had delivered. I ducked around them, rushed down the stone steps, and headed to the car.

Now, back to Aunt Lena's, where I started in the first place...

We walked into Aunt Lena's hallway as the clock struck one and into the living room, where Uncle Erastus, a big jolly man with a deep voice, was sitting in his leather chair reading the Sunday paper. Wonderful smells drifted in from the kitchen.

The dining room table was set and ready for all the serving dishes to be placed around. Aunt Lena always used rose patterned dinner plates, with crisp white linen napkins by their sides.

Uncle "Ras" asked us to hold hands while he said, *"Bless this food to the strength and nourishment of our bodies and us to thy service. In Christ name we pray. Amen."*

Since everyone had to go to church on Sunday, women cooked on Saturday. Aunt Lena baked a roast, made gravy, green beans, congealed fruit salad, homemade rolls and a cake. No meal at Aunt Lena's was ever complete without rice, so after church she whipped up a pot of fluffy white rice and heated the roast beef and gravy. I enjoyed everything put before me, all the while wondering what kind of cake lay beneath the aluminum covered cake plate on the sideboard.

My parents watched my manners like two beady eyed vultures sitting on the limb of a dead oak tree. I felt like a trapped chicken.

I got nervous as I started down the list of things I had to remember: Don't let your eyes be bigger than your stomach, don't take more than you can eat, eat everything on your plate, little children in China are starving to death, sit up straight, place your napkin in your lap, don't put your elbows on the table, chew with your mouth closed, and say please and thank you every time you are offered anything. Also, only speak when spoken to. When everyone has finished say, *Aunt Lena, thank you, I enjoyed the dinner.*

Believe me, I knew the routine and I knew my parents were keeping score. Not only was this the Bible Belt it was also the whuppin' belt. If my father was doing the whuppin', it was with a belt. If my mother was doing it, I could expect to go cut my own switch.

When dinner was over and I had made my *thank you, I enjoyed it* speech, I was allowed to go outside, if I was quiet. Anything that was fun had to wait until Monday.

I was wondering if I had passed the manners test and thinking how thankful I was that I hadn't been one of those little children that got drowned in the flood because somebody made God mad. Did God get mad and drown the Chinese too? Was he mad at the hungry little Chinese children and didn't let them have any rice?

The afternoon wore on, and as dusk settled in, it brought out hordes of mosquitoes and got me wondering, *why in heaven's, name did God let those pesky little things live to suck our blood and give us itchy whelps?*

I was sitting on the curb next to the street when I saw a white cloud forming and coming toward me. The seamless cloud of white smoke rose in the air, and I realized it was the bug spray truck coming for the mosquitoes. I sat there and let the fog cover me. I inhaled the white mist and let it fill my lungs, hoping it would cleanse me from the demons that lived inside me.

Right behind the bug spray truck came a car with a loud speaker on top. "This is evangelist Oliver B. Green coming to save you from spending eternity burning in hell. The devil is trying this very minute to get you to turn away from God, but I have come to bring you salvation. Accept Jesus Christ as your Lord and Savior tonight, right now, get down on your knees and repent. Ask God to forgive you for your sins.

"I will be conducting a revival meeting in a tent right off main street all next week. Come and be born again. Experience a laying on of hands that will heal your body of whatever ails you and make you whole again."

Then Oliver B. Green faded away into the fumes left behind by the bug spray truck.

When we got home, my behavior report was not too bad. I was spared a whuppin'.

After I put on my pajamas, I had to kneel down by my bed and perform my last Christian duty of the day. Being a Christian can wear a person out, but I said, "Now I lay me down to sleep, I pray the Lord my soul to keep, if I should die before I wake, I pray the Lord my soul to take."

I lay in bed a long time with a lot of scary stuff running around in my head, because now the possibility of dying in my sleep did not make me want to close my eyes.

The only good thing that happened all day was Aunt Lena's dinner, and especially the chocolate cake.

I wished I could have had a hug and a kiss. A lullaby would have been nice, until I remembered what I used to hear: *"Rock a bye baby in the tree top, when the wind blows the cradle will rock, when the bow breaks the cradle will fall, down will come baby, cradle and all."*

Well now, getting your brains bashed out on the ground beneath a tree is not a very comforting thought.

So I thought of the sandman. He wasn't a scary person. He was a nice old man with a sack of sand on his back. He wanted you to sleep well and have pleasant dreams. He sneaked up on you slowly and quietly and sprinkled sand in your eyes.

So my eyes got heavier and heavier until I couldn't hold them open any longer, and .......

## Go On and Cry

The year was 1945, a sunny April afternoon, and I had just come home from school, a carefree thirteen- year- old soul with nothing better to do than decide whether to roller-skate on the concrete portico at Sherwell's store--- or ride my bike around the neighborhood. I'd do anything to break the monotony of living in the country, where there was nothing much to do, and nobody much to do it with.

That afternoon I rode my bike past the flour mill, across the railroad tracks, past Dad Brown's store, the Post Office, and down a dirt road lined with houses rented by people at work in the mill. I could smell the grain that machines were grinding into flour and cornmeal. The machines would then pass the flour and cornmeal through a shoot into cloth sacks below, that were tied with twine and loaded into box cars, to be picked up by a freight train in the middle of the night.

Just as I passed the Bradshaw house, the screen door banged open like a shotgun blast, and Jack burst out yelling, "The President is dead!"

I slammed on my brakes and came to a screeching stop. The skidding tires made dirt and rocks fly up under my feet.

"How do you know?" I asked.

"It's on the radio. Go home and listen."

I was in shock and disbelief. The only news worse would have been if Jack had said God is dead. After all, next to God, our president was the most powerful person in the world. He had just gotten us through the great depression, putting people back to work building roads and bridges. He sent the Civilian Conservation Corps to our farm to plant hundreds of pine trees. Now I could climb to the top of those pines, making them sway back and forth like a ride at the county fair.

And to make matters worse, our country was in the middle of a war!

I rushed home and turned on the radio. Over the static, I heard: "The president died today in Warm Springs, Georgia. He had just finished lunch when he complained of a headache. The doctor who attended him stated that he suffered a cerebral hemorrhage and was pronounced dead at 3:30 P.M.

"Vice President Harry S. Truman is preparing to take the oath of office, and he will become our thirty third president."

My eyes filled with tears. Our president really was dead.

Four years earlier, I had been listening to music on the radio in Grandpa's car. I was all dressed up in my Sunday dress, my hair curled and combed to look my best as we headed to my uncle's house for lunch. My mind was focused on how hungry I was, and I hoped we would have my favorite chicken and dumplings, homemade yeast rolls, and a big slice of chocolate cake.

During that ride, my daydream had been ended with this broadcast:

"We interrupt this regularly scheduled program to bring you the following:

"This is Charles Daly reporting. The Japanese have just bombed Pearl Harbor. President Franklin Delano Roosevelt has declared this an act of war."

I felt fear and uncertainty coming from everyone in the car, and I saw the shock in their eyes. *The Japanese are coming to kill us,* I thought. I was scared. My Grandpa could do just about anything, but even he couldn't fix that.

Before long, our men went off to war. We were issued ration books of little stamps that we used for sugar, butter, gas and shoes. At school, we started each morning with a prayer for God to bless out country. We pledged allegiance to the flag, sang patriotic songs, and turned in pennies to buy war bonds. We came together, all of us, to do our part as we grieved for the loved ones who weren't coming back.

I was eight years old when FDR ran for a third term against Wendell Wilkie. Being a kid, I didn't have a dog in that fight, but I sure wished I did. I wanted Wilkie to win just because my parents voted for FDR. Back then, Southerners voted Democratic because it was a vote against the Party of Lincoln, the Republican who freed the slaves. My greatgrandmother, a feisty little lady who dressed in pretty dresses with a cameo brooch at the neckline, and wore her white hair pulled up into a bun on top of her head, said she would vote for a Democrat even if he was a black man or a yellow dog.

My father would do anything to keep the black man in his place, including hiding under a sheet and burning a cross in his yard. I wasn't too young to know what hate was, and I saw it all around me. I also knew love when I saw it, and that was what I got from the black woman who took care of me.

On voting day, the polling place was set up in Sherwell's store near the bib overalls, flannel shirts, and work boots. It was a wire frame covered by canvas, with a flap in front for privacy. My father pulled an ice cold Coke Cola from the drink box, got a pack of peanuts from a big glass jar, handed them to me, and pointed to a chair where I was supposed to wait while I watched the white folks vote.

Women were minorities, too. My father made my mother vote the way he told her. It hadn't been too many years since women fought long and hard to win the right to vote, but I watched my mother let him lead her into the booth and take it away. I might have been young, but I wasn't stupid.

It was cold the night of the election, and my mother made my favorite chipped beef on toast. She got out a bourbon soaked A & P fruit cake and cut a piece for each of us before we gathered around the radio to listen to the returns.

I had to keep quiet about my feelings, because really I wasn't supposed to have any. So I kept quiet and just listened until I was made to go to bed, hoping that my candidate,

Wilkie, had won. In the morning I had to face the truth – he lost.

Eventually, I came to love FDR and all he stood for, but now he was dead. Our first lady, Eleanor, felt free to speak her mind. She didn't let any man, even the President, take away her power. She became my idol. I didn't know a thing about Harry S. Truman, except that he had a wife named Bess.

Truman helped us move from war to a peaceful period, except that Russia was breathing down our necks.

In the next few years I forgot about politics and became more interested in other things- - such as boys. I graduated from high school and headed off to college, free at last from my tyrannical father. My main concern was whether my wool plaid skirts matched my green class jacket. I liked bouncing into the soda shop to order a milk shake and a hot dog, while listening to Johnny Ray sing *Cry* on the juke box:

"If your sweetheart sends a letter of goodbye, it's no secret you'll feel better if you cry. Sunshine can be found behind a cloudy sky, so hang your head down baby and go on and cry."

Finally, at long last, I got old enough to vote. General Dwight David Eisenhower ran against Adlai Stevenson. My father instructed me to vote for Adlai, because he was a

Democrat and kin to us. I never found out how we were related, and my father never found out that I voted for the handsome, personable, five star general who led our troops to victory in World War II.

In the parlor of our dorm, we gathered to watch the returns on TV, and my man won. Shortly after his inauguration, Eisenhower made a stop in a nearby town, and I cut classes to go hear his speech. I thought it might be the only time I was able to see a president in person, and it was.

Ten years later, I was captivated by John Fitzgerald Kennedy and his compassion for all the things I felt were right. I had lived through the big protest marches in Mississippi and Alabama, church bombings, hangings, beatings, sit-ins at lunch counters, cross burnings, attempts to integrate schools --- some of the worst atrocities committed against human beings since the Holocaust.

Martin Luther King, Jr. gave his *I Have a Dream* speech and cried out his famous *Free at last, free at last. Thank God Almighty, I'm free at last!* And for that, some stupid redneck shot him.

Then on November 22, 1963, I was sitting in front of the TV folding clothes, waiting for my children to come home from school, when Walter Cronkite said:

"We interrupt this regularly scheduled program with a special news report. The President has been shot in Dallas, Texas and has been taken to Parkland Hospital, where we were told that he has been administered the last rites by a Catholic Priest."

Several minutes later Cronkite said:

"Our correspondent in Texas, Dan Rather, has just informed us that the President has died."

Walter Cronkite cried.

Lyndon Baines Johnson took the oath of office soon after. He passed the Voting Rights Act, giving black men and women the right to vote. This angered those Southerners who still wanted to keep blacks oppressed, and because this happened on a Democrat's watch, the south turned Republican.

Back when my great-grandmother said she would vote for a Democrat, even if he was a black man, it was inconceivable that this could ever happen.

But in 2008, a dynamic young man ran for president. He had a white mother, a black father, and his name was Barack Obama. He got his black skin and his funny name from his African father. Some ignorant folks didn't care that he had a white mother and was raised by white grandparents, because even one drop of black pigment in your skin made you a black person, end of story.

People tried hard to discredit him by claiming he wasn't born in The United States, he was a Muslim, and he didn't love America enough.

Obama's mother wrote a book about the time when they lived in Indonesia, where the natives hated black people so much, they let their children throw rocks at Barack. She said, "Oh, that's okay, he's used to it." So Barack Obama learned early to be calm and turn the other cheek.

Free at last, free at last – not really. The fight for freedom and equality must be fought over and over. There will always be people who want to keep us chained to the past.

Things have changed since that thirteen- year -old girl skated on the concrete portico in front of the store, where black people couldn't vote, and black friends couldn't ride bikes or skate with little white girls. Then nobody thought it was even possible to have a black president.

I remember Melanie's song: "I've got a brand new pair of roller-skates, and you've got a brand new key. I think that we should get together and try them on and see. I've been looking around a while, you've got something for me. Oh, I've got a brand new pair of rollerskates, and you've got a brand new key. I think we should get together and try them on and see."

## In the Sweet By and By

The weathered old house sat deep in the woods, down a long, dusty, red dirt road. The steps needed repairing and so did the boards on the front porch. A swing dangled by one rusty chain holding up the left side. Flower pots on the steps held brown ferns that died long before old Mrs. Morgan did.

At 10:30 AM, the funeral car parked in front of the house. The driver helped Lucy Mae Morgan and her aunts, Janie and Rose, into the long black car that would take them to Ebenezer Baptist church.

Lucy Mae, a tall thin woman with straight salt and pepper hair, who had just turned fiftytwo, had never been to a funeral before, not even her father's. So to her, this was a grand occasion. She had on the thick, black stockings that she wore year round, a black dress they found in her mother's closet, a black lace shawl, and a black hat with a floppy brim. When she saw herself in the mirror, she giggled and said, "Oh my gosh, oh my gosh, now ain't that somethin'!"

Preacher Martin, a squinty eyed little man with crooked teeth, limp gray hair, and a black velvet robe, stood in the pulpit and said some really nice things about Lucy Mae's mother, who lay in a polished wooden casket in front of the pulpit.

Violet's head rested on a pink satin pillow, and her hands were crossed on a pink quilt that mostly covered the dress they put on her. A spray of pink roses lay on the foot of the casket, bearing a ribbon that said: *From your loving family,* in gold letters. Flower arrangements were all around, in wreathes, on stands, and in floor baskets. Each one had a bright ribbon and a card attached.

Some men from the funeral home closed the casket and took it behind the church to the cemetery. Lucy Mae planted her feet firmly in the red dirt as she watched them lower her mama into the ground. All the flowers were arranged in a semi-circle at the head of the grave. Lucy Mae loved the scent of the roses, lilies, and carnations that rolled across the cemetery. She loved the way the colorful ribbons sparkled in the sun and fluttered in the breeze. A dove cried its mournful sound from somewhere deep in the woods.

Janie said, "Lucy Mae, you may keep the ribbon that says: *From your loving family* as a remembrance of your mother."

Lucy Mae circled all the arrangements, smelling the flowers and rubbing her fingers over the colorful ribbons. Then she pulled out several flowers to take home.

The preacher and several people gave her a hug and said how sorry they were about her loss. They also told her how nice she looked, and what a pretty hat she was wearing. So Lucy Mae giggled and said, "Oh, my gosh, oh, my gosh, now ain't that somethin'!"

Not many people attended the funeral, since the Morgans hadn't been to church for many years. They more or less kept to themselves. It had been a very long time since anyone had actually seen Violet Morgan. Her sisters, Janie and Rose, took turns caring for both Violet and Lucy Mae, sometimes called "Loony Mae" by the locals. But Janie and Rose had families of their own and were anxious to return home.

That afternoon, the sisters discussed what was to become of Lucy Mae. Rose wanted to put her in a home, but Janie wouldn't hear of it, besides what home would take her?

They decided to ask, Gussie, Violet's former cook, to move in and take care of Lucy Mae. Gussie was getting up in age. She had arthritis in her knees, which caused a lot of pain and made it difficult for her to walk. Never the less,
Gussie agreed, knowing full well what problems lay ahead. After all, Gussie had helped raise Lucy Mae.

Lucy Mae had a routine she followed every afternoon. Well actually, everything she did all day was a routine. Any change was very upsetting, and no one wanted to be around Lucy Mae when that happened. She could throw a mean temper tantrum and yell words she'd learned from old man Morgan.

At 3:00 PM, she and her dog, Flossie, walked to the post office. And every afternoon she said, "Ollie, did the mail train come? Did I get any mail?" And every afternoon, Ollie said, "No mail today, Lucy Mae."

Lucy would turn to Flossie and say, "Oh my gosh, oh my gosh, now ain't that somethin'! No mail today, Flossie. Let's go to the store."

Flossie would wag her tail and follow Lucy Mae to the store, where she would get a Pepsi and a candy bar for herself, and a slice of cheese for the dog. The clerk put everything on Janie's charge account.

Next Lucy Mae sat on the bench in a spot near the front window, drinking her Pepsi, eating her candy and talking to Flossie until 4:30 PM, when she said, "Oh my gosh, oh my gosh ain't that somethin'! Flossie it's time to go." The dog was so familiar with the routine, she got up and headed to the door.

One day on the way home, as they passed the church, the sign out front said *Shuford funeral Thursday, 11:00 AM.*

"Oh my gosh, oh my gosh, now ain't that somethin', Flossie? "That old man Shuford died!"

She and Flossie trudged down the red ruts in the driveway and arrived home at 5:00 PM. Gussie had dinner ready right on schedule at 6:00 PM. Lucy Mae would only eat from her very own pink plate, with a likeness of Queen Elizabeth in the center and a gold border on the rim.

After dinner, Gussie read Bible stories from an old worn book that Lucy Mae got for Christmas when she was six years old. She went to bed at 9:00 PM, and would only wear her night gown with little angels on it, so thin you could see right through it.

Thursday morning Lucy put on her black funeral dress, shawl, hat, and black stockings with her lace up shoes and walked to the church for the Shuford funeral.

One of the ushers saw her coming and said, "Lord God, here comes Loony Mae.

Where in the name of heaven are we going to seat her?"

They didn't have to worry, because Lucy Mae had her seat all picked out. It became her spot for every funeral held in Ebenezer Baptist Church after that.

Mr. Shuford was lying in a casket lined with blue satin. There were so many pretty flowers. She loved the heart -shaped wreath of red roses with a red ribbon that said: *Love, Sissy and family.* She loved the gladiolas with a big sequin- covered yellow ribbon that fell almost to the floor.

That afternoon at 3:00 PM, when she and Flossie headed out the door for the post office, the sky was beginning to turn gray.

Gussie said, "Lucy Mae, it look like it's gonna rain. You better stay home."

"Gussie, you know I need to be at the Post Office at 3:00 to get my mail."

"Yeah right. When was the last time you got any mail?"

"I'll get some today--- maybe a letter from Aunt Janie or Aunt Rose."

"Well, you ain't nothin' if you ain't hard-headed, so you go on. Don't you come back in here soaking wet, though, you and that nasty- smellin' dog. I ain't puttin' up with much more of your foolishness. I done told you, I can go off and leave your crazy ass here by yourself." "I don't care. Go on and leave, Gussie."

When they arrived at the post office, the sky was pretty dark.

"Did the mail train come, Ollie?"

"Yes, ma'am."

"Did I get any mail?"

"No, you didn't, Lucy Mae. But listen, we're fixin' to have a storm. You need to get yourself home as soon as you can."

"Well, I ain't been to the store yet."

"Go home, Lucy Mae."

It was already sprinkling when Lucy and Flossie reached the store. The clerk handed her the usual purchase, and said, "Lucy Mae that dog stinks. You need to get her out of here."

"Well, she ain't leavin' till I do, and I ain't had my Pepsi and candy yet."

She walked over to the bench and sat in her usual spot, with Flossie at her feet.

"Flossie don't pay him no mind. He ain't the boss of me or you. Just eat your cheese." When she left at 4:30 PM, it was still raining. She got to the church and decided to stop in and wait for the rain to let up.

"Flossie, you ain't never been in a church. This is where they bring dead people. They put them right under the pulpit in a shiny box. People give them flowers and they sing sad songs and cry a lot. They brought Mama in here. I didn't cry, but Aunt Janie and Aunt Rose did some. Come on. I'll take you out and show you where they put dead people in the ground."

When they got home, Lucy Mae and Flossie tracked mud all over the porch and down the hall. Gussie, with her hair tied up in a red rag and wearing her apron made from bleached sugar sacks, started screaming when the two came into the kitchen.

"Didn't I tell you to stay home? But no, you don't do nothing but just what you want to do. Now I got to mop that floor, and my knees is just killing me. I'm calling your aunt Janie tonight and telling her I just can't hardly stand your meanness no more. Git that dog outta
here before I kill it."

Gussie got out Lucy Mae's plate with Queen Elizabeth's picture on it and put a baked sweet potato, a pork chop, and piece of corn bread right over the Queen's face.

"You sit there and eat, and don't say nothin' to me. You gettin' on my nerves real bad."

The next morning, Lucy Mae took some pork chop scraps out on the back porch for Flossie. She called and called, but the dog never came.

Gussie said, "Don't worry, she's probably out catching rabbits. And she's so full of rabbit, she don't want this stuff we give her."

Lucy Mae moped around the house all day, and later Gussie said, "Lucy, I think that dog just went off and died."

"My dog ain't dead. I just heard her barking down behind the barn. She'll be back when she gets ready."

But Flossie wasn't back when Lucy Mae was set to go to the post office, at 3:00 PM. Ignoring her missing pet, Lucy Mae said, "Gussie, me and Flossie are leaving to go get my mail. Come on Flossie, let's go!"

*Good Lord in heaven, that girl done started talkin' to a dead dog,* thought Gussie.

Lucy Mae arrived right at 3:00 PM and asked for her mail.

"You ain't got none," said Ollie. "Just like I said yesterday, and the day before that, and the day before that---- you ain't got no mail, Lucy Mae."

"Oh my gosh, oh my gosh, now ain't' that somethin'. Flossie, let's go. We ain't got no mail today."

"Wait a minute, Lucy Mae, Flossie didn't come in here with you."

"She sure did. She's right here beside me. Let's go, Flossie."

Lucy Mae pushed her straight hair behind her ears and headed across the road in her black wool stockings and black lace up shoes, talking to Flossie all the way.

She didn't miss a single funeral at Ebenezer Baptist church that year. When she entered the church, everyone said, "Here comes Looney Mae, dressed like a big black buzzard."

One day Preacher Martin drove his old Chevrolet into the woods, down the long bumpy driveway to the Morgan house. He climbed the broken steps and knocked.

Lucy Mae answered the door.

The preacher said, "May I come in? I need to have a word with you."

Lucy Mae said, "Well wait a minute 'til I get Flossie out of the way. Move Flossie, so the preacher can come in."

The preacher wasn't surprised. He had heard that she talked to her dead dog. He also knew Lucy attended all the funerals at Ebenezer, and that the members called her "the black buzzard".

Preacher Martin took a seat in an old lumpy chair by the window. He cleared his throat and said, "We've had some very mysterious things happening at our church this past year. It seems someone has been visiting the cemetery after almost every funeral. They've been messing with the floral arrangements. Sometimes we find flowers missing, sometimes we find flowers from one wreath stuck into another wreath and ribbons from one arrangement placed on another. Many times, the ribbons are actually missing."

Lucy Mae fidgeted around in her chair and pushed her hair behind her ears.

Gussie cleared her throat and said, "Lucy Mae, what do you know about this?

"Oh, my gosh, oh my gosh, now ain't that somethin'?"

"You ain't answering my question. What do you know?"

"Well, I'm thinkin' I don't know much."

"That means you know *something.* Exactly what do you know?" Gussie demanded.

"Well, me and Flossie do go look at the flowers. She likes the pretty ribbons, and sometimes I give her one to bring home."

"And do you know where Flossie puts them?" Preacher Martin asked.

"Usually in the tool shed," answered Lucy Mae.

"Would you take me there and show me?"

The three of them walked behind the house to the tool shed. When they opened the door, the most wonderful odor imaginable drifted through.

The walls were covered with ribbons. Ribbons of all colors. There were big bows and small bows. Ribbons that said: *From all your children, From your grandchildren, From your sister Mary, From Margaret and Pete, From your Sunday School Class, From Circle Number Five, From Reeves Lumber Mill.*

Baskets holding dead flowers were scattered around the shed. Wreaths on easels were arranged against the back wall, and there was a shelf lined with fruit jars. Each jar held a different color rose petal.

It was a potpourri heaven.

Gussie said, "Oh, sweet Jesus!"

Finally Preacher Martin spoke. "Lucy Mae, what do you have to say about all this?

She giggled and giggled and said, "Oh my gosh, oh my gosh, now ain't that somethin'?"

# Hide-Away Hell

Fifteen more minutes! It was the last day of school and I was squirming around in my desk with unbearable impatience. I watched the hands on the clock move to 2:45 PM, fifteen more minutes 'til the bell rang, releasing us for two months of fun and freedom.

A report card guaranteeing my promotion to the tenth grade was clutched tightly in my hand, and I had one foot in the isle ready to take flight. Soon there would be whoopin' and hollerin' and a stampede down the stairs and across the parking lot to the big orange buses waiting to take us home.

Early the next morning, my mother, my little sister, Janet, and I were going to our cottage at Wrightsville Beach to begin our summer vacation. Daddy had to stay behind to mind his store, while our older brother, Cliff, was enrolled in summer classes at The University of North Carolina in Chapel Hill.

It was 1946. The war was over, our soldiers were coming home, gas rationing had ended and it was time to celebrate.

Our cottage was on Salisbury Street, the very same street as the LUMINA, also called "The Pleasure Palace of the South." It had been shut down during the war. The threat of German attack required low light, dimouts and beach blackouts. But now, the eight foot high LUMINA glittered once again, over the water and out to the sea.

The LUMINA was a 25,000 square foot structure with a promenade on the first floor where you could go bowling, see a movie, or win a kewpie doll or stuffed animal at a shooting gallery. You could buy a milk shake and a hotdog covered with mustard, onions, and chili.

The second floor had a restaurant, a dance hall, and a balcony where big bands from all over the country came to play. I had learned to Shag that year and was dying to join the teens who danced into the night. Mama and Daddy didn't let me and Janet go there much, but we could hear the bands from our cottage.

In preparation for the vacation, Mama spent hours at her sewing machine making us shorts and blouses from the material she bought at Belk department store. We washed and ironed our clothes, then packed them along with our bathing suits, some library books, Janet's watercolors, and the embroidery pieces I was working on. We already had a bookcase filled with games and puzzles in the cottage, so we didn't need to take those things.

Mama packed a box of sheets, towels and all kinds of food she had purchased at our family store. Our cook, Effie, made a picnic lunch for us to eat on the way. I put on the new red shorts and halter Mama made, and Janet wore her new navy blue outfit.

Daddy drove the car to the pumps at our store, filled the gas tank, and said, "Y'all be careful now. I'll join you later." Then we on the road without a care in the world... we thought.

We rolled into Wrightsville Beach about 4:30 PM and drove down Salisbury Street to our little cottage, with the sign on the front that read: *Harris Family Hide-A-Way.*

When I stepped out of the car onto the driveway covered with broken oyster shells, the smell of salt air and the sound of waves crashing against the shore made me want to shout with joy. I was so excited, I could hardly stand it, although my Mama had already warned us to not even think about going to the beach until we had unpacked and put everything away.

I was the first one out of the car. I entered the screened porch, ready to place the key in the cottage door, when I saw that it was already unlocked. Something wasn't right. When I opened the door and saw blood on the floor, I screamed to high heaven.

The place had been ransacked! There were dirty glasses in the kitchen sink, food wrappers on the cabinet. Empty beer cans and bourbon bottles were scattered everywhere. The jar of spare change we kept on the kitchen counter was empty, and some bedspreads were wadded up and thrown on the floor.

Mama said, "Don't touch anything. Get in the car. We have to go down to the Food Mart to call the police and your father."

Two policemen, Chief Wallace and Sergeant Adams, showed up in about thirty minutes. We all had to sit out on the porch while they investigated. The two men went through every room and took photos of the blood.

In the meantime, I heard people talking, laughing, and having a really good time over at the pavilion. Visions of girls doing the Shag with good looking boys made me dizzy as I sat there with my sister and mother, just feeling mad as hell.

Johnnie Mercer was singing on the Lumina balcony that evening. It wasn't long before he started singing *In the Cool, Cool of the Evening, That old Black Magic, Come Rain or Come Shine, One for My Baby,* and *Let's Take the Long Way Home.*

Finally, the police came out to talk to mother. "Mrs. Harris, when was the last time you were here, and when was your husband last here? Does he ever come here without you, maybe to go fishing? Are there any other members in your family?"

"Yes, I have a son, Cliff," Mama said.

"Where is he now?"

"He's in summer school at Chapel Hill. Next year he'll be going to law school."

"Does he ever come here without you?"

"He's not supposed to come without our permission." Mama frowned.

"Do you rent the cottage, or let any friends or other family members use it?" asked the Chief.

"No," Mama said.

When the police left, we were too tired, hungry, and stressed to unpack the car or clean up the filth the intruders, whoever they were, had left behind. But we did it anyway. Mama was so irritable, you would think Janet and I were the ones who made the mess in the first place.

It was really late by the time we got the cottage back in shape. Thank goodness the police had cleaned the blood off the floor before they left. Janet was holding back tears when she asked Mama who she thought got murdered.

Mama said, "Oh, don't you worry about that. It was probably some tramp who didn't belong around here anyway."

I put clean sheets on my bed, took a bath, and climbed into my pajamas. But I was too scared to sleep. I really needed to open the window to let in the cool ocean breeze, but I was afraid someone might crawl in through that window. After all, some awful people had been here and maybe murdered someone. Maybe they slept in my bed, or killed somebody in my bed, and then dragged the body through the cottage and outside.

My lord, what a way to start a summer vacation! Daddy was coming down tomorrow. He wanted to see things for himself and talk to the police. We would feel safer then. He would get all this straightened out. That's what I was telling myself, when I finally went to sleep.

Mama made pancakes for breakfast, and then took us down to the Food Mart to blow up our rafts at the air pump. We were allowed go out on the beach and stay as long as we wanted. Mama left food in the refrigerator for sandwiches when we got hungry, and Daddy was scheduled to arrive about 1:00 PM to talk to the police.

It was 2:00 PM when the police came and questioned Daddy. They asked when was the last time he had been here, the last time Cliff had been here, and when had Daddy last talked to Cliff.

"Mr. Harris, I hate to tell you this, but we found a body of a young man on the beach several days ago, and he's still unidentified." Chief Wallace sadly shook his head. "The victim suffered a serious head wound that looks very suspicious. We're going to stay on top of it.

"We also contacted UNC Chapel Hill and learned that your son has not attended classes in two weeks. We may ask you to go to the morgue, to see if you can identify the body."

I was in the kitchen making myself a ham sandwich when Mama started screaming.

Daddy said, "For god sake, Carol, stop assuming the worst. Getting hysterical isn't going to solve a damn thing now."

"Well, you know Cliff drinks too much...." Mama whimpered. "If he's not at school, where is he? Just put two and two together. He must have come here with some friends, had one of his drinking parties, and somebody killed him! Now he's in the morgue."

But Daddy didn't seem concerned, just mad. "Well, if I'm paying for him to be in school at Carolina, and if he's not there, I'll kill him myself."

I took my ham sandwich and Coke Cola out on the screened porch and tried to eat in peace. But it wasn't easy with my mama screaming because she thought she had a dead son, and my daddy screaming that mama didn't know any such thing, so she should just shut up about it.

Then my sister Janet started crying. "Maryanne, is Cliff is dead? Who do you think killed him?"

I told her not to worry, that he would turn up safe and sound. I also tried to keep her from knowing how worried I was.

Eventually Mama went to bed, but we could hear her crying and praying all night.

The next morning, Daddy took his fishing rod, got in his truck, slammed the door and left.

I put on my new bathing suit with sunflowers on it, and then Janet and I went out on the beach. I lay down on a towel. I had already streaked my hair with peroxide, hoping to bleach it, and smeared myself with Johnson's baby oil.

I rolled over on my stomach and tried to cover my ears, so I couldn't hear all the laughter coming from the pavilion. I was trying to figure out how to get Mama and Daddy to let me go to the pavilion after supper. It wasn't going to happen, and I already knew it. In fact, I knew exactly what my Mama would say: "Marianne Harris, your brother may be dead, and you want to go dancing?"

After I washed the supper dishes, my sister and I went out on the porch. Janet was rubbing Noxzema on my sunburned back when I heard the band start up – *GI Jive, Too Marvelous for Words, The Atchison, Topeka and the Santa Fe* and *Accentuate the Positive.* Janet was crying, and I was trying not to.

Chief Watson showed up early the next morning and said the body had been identified, and the victim's name was Jack Cook. "Does that name ring a bell, Mr. Harris?"

"Well, I'm not sure. How about you, Carol?"

Mama gasped and blurted out, "Oh my god! Yes, he was a friend of Cliff's."

"The autopsy report hasn't come back yet, but we are considering your son a person of interest," said Chief Watson.

"What are you saying, Chief Watson?" Mama asked.

"We're investigating a murder and looking for a possible suspect, so we need to talk to your son," he said. "I'll be back in touch, ma'am."

After Chief Watson left, Mama ran to her bedroom and slammed the door. I could hear her sobbing into her pillow.

Janet said, "Marianne, that's good news that Cliff's not dead, right?"

I didn't know what to say.

Eventually, Daddy came out of the bedroom. "Marianne, I'm taking your mama to the doctor to get something for her nerves. Stay inside the house in case the police come back. Take good care of Janet, and please prepare the meals until we get this matter resolved."

That night I finished slicing the ham, got out the Tupperware bowl of potato salad we brought down in the cooler, sliced some tomatoes and cucumbers and the chocolate pound cake Effie baked. I took Mama some food, but her pills had knocked her out for the night. I washed the dishes, cleaned the kitchen real good, and Janet and I were just starting Chinese checkers when the band began playing down the street. I got up and shut the door. I just couldn't bear to hear it.

Chief Watson appeared early the next morning, pounding on the door just as I was putting a platter of eggs and bacon on the table. Daddy went to let him in. Mama was still in bed and so out of it, she couldn't get up had she wanted to.

"Good morning, Mr. Harris," the chief said.

"What the hell is good about it?" Daddy grumbled.

"Actually, not much." Chief Watson agreed. "We've received another missing person report, this time for a girl named Jessie Mason from Ashe County. She's been gone over a week, and she was supposed to be attending summer school at Chapel Hill. Her parents told the police she was a close friend of your son's, so we think they may be together. Here's my card. If you hear anything, call me at this number."

Again, as soon as Chief Watson left, Daddy got his fishing rod, threw it in the back of the truck and left.

"Janet, put on your swim suit," I told my little sister. "Come hell or high water, we're going out on the beach until lunch, and then we're going to the pavilion for a hotdog and milkshake."

We hadn't been on the beach long before I saw storm clouds hanging far out at sea. I watched as they moved closer and closer, and it got darker and darker. Janet and I gathered our things and made it to the cottage just before the rain came.

We made peanut butter and jelly sandwiches, then spent the whole afternoon reading, playing Old Maid, and listening to the slow drizzling rain.

While I tried to act cheerful, I was really afraid of what might have happened to Cliff. I was even more worried about what would happen when Daddy found him.

"What if they can't find Cliff, Marianne?" Janet asked.

"If ifs, ands, and buts were candy and nuts, we'd all have a Merry Christmas," I said.

"Well it's not Christmas." Janet didn't get it.

"No, it's June. It's hot and humid, my back is sunburned, and all we can do is sit around and wait."

After I cleaned up the supper dishes, I walked out on the porch just in time to hear the band strike up *Stormy Weather*. I went straight to my bedroom, crawled in bed and pulled the covers over my head.

The next morning, Chief Watson came to tell us that Jack Cook's autopsy report revealed an excessive amount of alcohol in his bloodstream. In his drunken state, the boy had apparently fallen off the Johnnie Mercer Pier and hit his head on a piling, before falling into the water.

"Your son probably hosted a party in your cottage which included some heavy drinking. Right now we can't charge him with any crime, and we can't account for the blood on your floor. We may know more when we locate Jessie Mason, though. I know your son is running away from something, and he's afraid of getting caught."

"Hell!" Daddy cursed. "Cliff better be damn scared. He's going to pay back every penny he's costing me." With that, he stomped out to his truck, scattering oyster shells everywhere as he skidded out the driveway.

It was late afternoon when Daddy came back. He looked plumb worn out when he dragged in with a six-pack of beer. He took the opener from the kitchen drawer and popped one before he collapsed into a chair.

He looked at Mama and said, "Well, Carol, you can stop worrying. Your son is alive and well."

Mama started crying and thanking Jesus.

I was thinking, *best hold your tears 'til we hear the rest of the story.*

"I spent most of the day at the police station." Daddy sighed. "I got the locals to ask the police in Ashe County to check our mountain cabin, and just as I suspected, Cliff was there with Jessie Mason, who is five months pregnant. You can probably guess who the father is."

Daddy looked totally disgusted. "Cliff and Jesse came here first trying to decide what to do, then Jack and two other boys joined them to celebrate the end of school. They were in the pavilion drinking and dancing for a while before walking out on the pier. Jack and one of the boys started fighting, and Jack fell over into the water.

"Someone on the pier called the police. The kids were so scared, they ran back to the cottage, grabbed their belongings, and took off. Turns out the blood on the floor came from Cliff cutting his hand on a broken beer bottle...

"After that, Cliff drove Jessie to her parents' home in Ashe County expecting to leave her there, but when her parents realized she was pregnant, they told her she had embarrassed them so badly, they wanted her to leave and never come back.

"Next, Cliff took Jesse to our mountain cabin, and they've been hiding out there ever since, trying to figure out what to do next."        "Oh, my god, what is Clifford going to do?" Mama wailed.

"He's on the way home as we speak, bringing Jessie Mason and your unborn grandchild with him."

"But I'm not ready to be a grandmother! Cliff was going to law school, and then he was supposed to marry a nice girl in a big church wedding.  This is so embarrassing. Isn't there anything we can do?"

"Well, Carol, the first thing you can do is throw away your damned nerve pills. Then pack your clothes, go home, and meet your soon –to- be daughter-in-law."

After Daddy's pronouncement, Mama was crying and so was Janet.  I got Janet an ice cream sandwich and took her out on the porch.

Janet whined, "And all this time, I've been so worried.  First I thought Cliff was dead. Then I thought he killed Jack, and that the police were chasing him in the mountains with blood hounds, and maybe they would shoot him or put him in prison. And then I thought Mama was having a nervous breakdown, and Daddy would put her in a mental hospital. And I didn't know what would happen to us. Now I'm just mad as hell!"

"Yeah, I know how you feel," I mumbled as I went into the bedroom to pack my clothes.

## Radio Romance

"Doppler radar shows shower activity west of Charlotte over Caldwell County on this Monday night. It's clear over Charlotte and 72 degrees. Tomorrow should be sunny and 75 degrees, and to our south--- down around Chester and Cheraw---it will be partly cloudy and 75 degrees. This is WBT 1110 in Charlotte, North Carolina.

Stay tuned for *Hello Henry*...."

***

"Honk, Honk! This is Goose Queen Charlotte saying hello to our listeners up and down eastern seaboard, and this is Henry Hogan saying welcome! We want to hear from you. Tell us what's on your mind tonight. We want to hear about your day and take requests for your favorite songs, so pick up the phone and give us a call.

"We'll start your night off with Steely Dan playing *Do It Again....*"

> *Then you love a little wild one and she brings you only sorrow.*
>
> *All the time you know she's smilin', you'll be on your knees tomorrow.*
>
> *Yeah, you go back, Jack do it again, wheel turnin' 'round and 'round.*
>
> *You go back Jack, do it again...*

"Hello, Henry. My name is Claudia, from Concord, and I'm missing my boyfriend so much. His name is Jason, and he's at North Carolina State. Will you play *Don't Go Breaking My Heart* by Elton John?"

"Okay, Claudia. We're sending this song to you, Jason--- all the way to Raleigh. So don't break this girl's heart, pal!"

> *Nobody knows it... when I was down, I was your clown.*
>
> *Nobody knows it right from the start,*
>
> *I gave you my heart, I gave you my heart,*

*So don't go breaking my heart.*

"Hello Henry, this is Alma, from Alabama".

"My gosh, Miss Alma! We've missed you. Haven't heard from you in a coon's age."

"Well, I been kinda laid up for a while. Just ain't been well at all."

"I'm sorry to hear that, young lady. Hope you're feeling better."

"Well, yeah, I went fishin' yesterday. Caught me a mess of crappy. Fried 'em up last night. They was real good."

"How's the weather down there, Miss Alma?"

"It's good. Been kinda cool, but sunny. Can't complain none about the weather."

'Now, young lady, don't you wait so long to call again. And here is Lynyard Skynyrd to sing this song just for you..."

> *Sweet home Alabama, where the skies are so blue.*

> *Sweet home Alabama, Lord, I'm coming home to you.*

"Hello, this is Henry."

"Hello, my name is Lee. I'm a second grade school teacher, and I just moved to Charlotte. I guess to tell the truth, I'm kind of homesick. I just wanted to tell you how much I enjoy your program. I turn you on every night, and your familiar voice gives me something to look forward to."

"That's real nice to hear. Welcome to Charlotte, Lee. Thanks for calling. I hope Charlotte will soon feel like your home."

\*\*\*

This is WBT 1110, and Jim McSwaim broadcasting this Tuesday night, bringing you the latest weather forecast... Presently we are experiencing light showers over most of the Charlotte area, and it's 71 degrees. There is heavy rain to the east of us, down toward Albemarle. But most of our viewing area should be fair and sunny tomorrow. Now stay tuned for *Hello Henry...*"

\*\*\*

"Welcome to my friends from up and down the eastern seaboard, and to all in between. This is Henry. I'm waiting for you to call and tell me what's on your mind tonight...."

"Hello, this is Henry."

"Henry, this is John, from Charlotte. Please play *Best of My Love* for my girlfriend, Ann, who is a freshman at UNCG."

"Will do, pal. Ann, here come The Eagles, flying all the way to Greensboro..."

*Every night, I'm lying in bed, holding you close in my dreams,*

*Thinkin' about all the things that we said and comin' apart at the seams.*

*We try to talk it over, but the words come out too rough.*

*I know you were trying to give me the best of your love.*

"Hello, Henry, my name is Eddy, and I'm from Charlotte. Please play a song for Lee. She called in last night--- a teacher who just moved to Charlotte--- and she was feeling homesick."

"What shall I play for Lee?"

"*Lean on Me,* by Bill Withers."

"Did you hear that, Lee? Looks like you've got a friend in Eddy. This is for *you,* young lady..."

*Lean on me, when you're not*

strong,          *and I'll be your friend,*

*I'll help you carry on,          for it won't*

*be long*

*'til I need somebody to lean on.*

***

Lee was lying in bed in the dark, and couldn't believe it when someone requested a song for her. She lay awake a long time wondering if maybe the caller was talking about some other Lee, some other school teacher who had just moved here... but it seemed pretty unlikely. She didn't know anyone named Eddy--- maybe someone from her past? It made her feel kind of special, though, so perhaps she would dedicate a song to him. She thought about it for a long time before she was able to fall asleep.

The next night, she turned on her radio and poured herself a glass of wine, trying to relax enough to get up the nerve to pick up the phone...

"Hello, this is Henry."

"Henry, this is Lee. I would like you to play a song for Eddy."

"Sure thing. What would you like me to send out to Eddy?"

"*I Can See Clearly Now,* by Jimmy Cliff."

"Will do. This song is especially for you, Eddy."

*I can see clearly now, the rain is gone.*

*I can see clearly, no obstacles in my way.*

*Gone are the dark clouds that kept me down.*

*It's gonna be a bright, bright, sunshiny day."*

***

Lee lay in her dark room and figured Eddy probably didn't hear the dedication. Maybe he had just been listening that one time. Or maybe he was a weirdo--- a- pervert. She turned out the light and went to sleep.

The next night, Thursday, she finished dinner early, graded some papers, took a shower, put on her pajamas, crawled into bed, and turned on the radio. Henry was getting his usual calls. Many people were complaining about the School Board, and some were gripping about zoning. Then came a call from Miss Alma, from Alabama. Lee was beginning to doze a little when she heard:

"Hello, Henry, this is Eddy. I want you to play a song for Lee."

"What's it going to be, Eddy?"

"*Night Fever,* by the Bee Gees."

*On the waves of the air, there is dancin' out there.*

*If it's somethin' we can share, we can steal it.*

*And that sweet city woman, she moves through the light,      controlling my mind and my soul.*

*When you reach out for me, yeah, and the feelin' is right,      then I get night fever, night fever.*

\*\*\*

The following Friday night, after a rough week of loud children, Lee was ready to relax. She wanted to send a song to Eddy, so she started calling early, but the line was busy for a whole hour. She listened to callers complaining about this and that, and a few lonely people just wanting to talk--- probably like her, with nothing better to do.

She finally got through at 9:15 PM and asked Henry to dedicate *Dream Weaver* to Eddy.

*I have just closed my eyes again,*

*climbed aboard the dream weaver train.*

*Driver take away my worries today and leave tomorrow behind.*

*Ooh dream weaver, I believe you can get me through the night.*

The song had just finished, when Lee heard Henry say:

"Hello Eddy, heard your song, did you?"

"I did, and I want you to play my very favorite song for Lee. I wouldn't ask you to do it for just anybody, but it's for Lee. Please play *White Azaleas,* by Eddy Arnold. I was named for Eddy Arnold, and he sings it better than anyone."

*When the white azaleas start blooming, I'll come back to you.*

*When spring's in the air with its freshness so rare,  we'll make our dreams come true.*

*When the white azaleas start blooming in those mountains so high,*

*  we'll build a nest where we'll find happiness, sweetheart,*

*  for only you and I.*

*When the white azaleas start blooming,*

*I'll come back to you.*

***

The following Monday, Lee dedicated *This Song's for You*, by Elton John.

*If I was a sculptor but then again no*

*or a man who makes potions in a traveling show –*

*oh, I know it's not much but it's the best I can do.*

*My gift is my song, and this song's for you.*

Lee listened all week for a response from Eddy, but he didn't call in. She couldn't believe what was happening to her. She was missing this person--- this perverted man who was trying to--- well god knows what he

was trying to do. It was just plain crazy---
she was crazy. She was a pathetic person
who needed to get a life.

By Friday, she decided to call in one
more time, then stop. No more of that
stupidity.

"Hello, this is Henry."

"Hello, Henry, this is Lee. Would you
play *White Azaleas* for Eddy?"

"Sure thing, young lady. Eddy, this
one's for you, pal..."

*When the white azaleas start blooming,*

*I'll come back to you.*

*When spring's in the air,*
*with its freshness so rare,*
*we'll make our dreams come*
*true.*

***

Lee decided she would listen on
Monday-- but she had definitely
called in for the very last time. She
had detached from this silliness once
and for all, but then she heard:
"Hello, Henry. This is Eddy."

"Well, welcome back, pal. Been
missing you here. You been doin' okay?"

"Yeah, a lot better now. Will you please play *White Azaleas* for Lee?"

"Sure, here we go again. Lee, this song's for you, young lady."

*Yeah,* Lee thought. *Thanks, that's just great. But I'm movin' on. So Long, Eddy.*

***

The kids were loaded on the buses and on their way home for the week-end, when Lee went back to her room and collapsed at her desk. The intercom came on and the secretary said, "Lee, some flowers have just been delivered for you."

"Are you sure they are for me?"

"Your name's on the card. It's a pot of white azaleas, from Andrews Florist, 127 North Tryon Street. It doesn't say who sent them."

The next Friday, a dozen red roses were delivered, again without the name of the sender. The next week, a mixed arrangement arrived, and by that time, Lee had decided to go the Andrews Florist and get to the bottom of the craziness.

The florist shop was a quaint little place that had been there for years. The building was painted green, and the sign over the door read: *Andrews Florist – since 1970.* The words were encircled in a vine-like wreath sprinkled with purple violets.

A little bell rang as Lee opened the door and walked up to the counter.

A young woman said, "May I help you?"

"My name is Lee, and I've been getting flowers from here every week. They never include the name of the sender. Do you have any idea who's doing it?"

"Sure, it's Eddy."

"Eddy who?"

"Eddy Andrews, the owner."

"May I speak to him, please?"

"He's not here today."

The next Friday, Andrews Florist delivered pink peonies.

Lee drove to the florist, this time determined to find Eddy Andrews. She walked in and pretended to be browsing through a rack of greeting cards. She could see through a window into the work area, where a man was working on a funeral wreath.

He wiped his hands on the blue and white stripped apron tied around his waist and approached her. He wore a *Grateful Dead* tee shirt his light blonde hair was tied back in a ponytail. He seemed to be the last remaining hippie this side of San Francisco.

"May I help you?" he asked.

Lee wanted a little more time to check him out before walking out the door. "I'm looking for a get well card," she said.

Just then, the bell rang and the door was flung open by a little boy with curly black hair and brown skin. He threw a book bag on a chair and said, "Dad, I'm hungry."

"There are drinks in the cooler and snacks on the counter. How was school today?" the hippie said.

"I made two goals in basketball practice."

*So*, she thought, *this man who dedicates sweet songs and sends beautiful flowers to me has a son and a wife at home. Well, I'm ready to tell the two-timing jerk where to go.*

Determined to let the creep know what she thought of him, she said, "May I speak to Eddy, please?"

"I'm Eddy."

In the meanest voice she could find, she said, "Well, I'm Lee."

He looked shocked and froze for a minute. "Lee, gosh, what a surprise!" he said nervously.

"C.J., come meet my friend." The little boy came in with a hand full of cookies.

"This is my son," Eddy said.

"Lee, please come in the back, and I'll make you a cup of tea. We'll also have some cookies if the kid didn't eat all of them."

The room was filled with the scent of sweet smelling blossoms that peered at her from behind the cooler doors.

Eddy turned to a girl working at a table. "Alice, finish the wreath I started and load the truck with all the flowers going to the funeral home. C.J., ride along with Alice and help her unload. Hurry up now, visitation starts at 7:00 PM sharp."

Eddy put a tea kettle on a hot plate, and in a few minutes, they were drinking Genmai with honey and lemon.

He seemed nervous and uncomfortable, as though he didn't know what to say.

Finally, Lee said, "I'm sorry to barge in on you at such a busy time."

"Oh, no it's okay. I'm glad to finally meet you."

In a few minutes, they were able to relax and laugh about their calls to Hello Henry.

When Alice and C.J. returned, Eddy sent his son down the street to pick up some Chinese food he had ordered, and he insisted that Lee follow him home and join him for supper.

They ate on his patio and watched C.J. and a friend shoot basketball in the driveway.

"My wife just left us one day," Eddy said. "C.J. was just a baby, so he doesn't remember her at all. She was a drug addict, you see. After two years waiting, hoping she'd come home and we'd get her some help, I finally gave up and filed for divorce. I'm afraid she's probably dead by now."

By the time Lee left, they were laughing together like two old friends. Eddy told her to turn on *Hello Henry* when she got home, and he would request a special song for her.

After that, they were together a lot, and Lee finally admitted to herself that she was in love with this wonderful hippie man who doted on his son. They had dinner together almost every night. She learned to cook things that C.J. liked, and afterwards helped him with his homework.

One night at dinner, Eddy suddenly closed his eyes and was still for a few minutes. Lee thought it was strange, but didn't say anything. But then, she began to notice it happening more often.

"Eddy, I'm worried about you," she said. "You seem to be having little seizures."

"Lee, I haven't been honest with you, and I'm so sorry. I haven't been this happy in a long time, and selfishly, I wanted to make it last as long as I could. You see, I have brain cancer.

"After the doctor told me it was a possibility, I couldn't fall asleep that night, and that's when I tuned in to *Hello Henry* and heard your voice. I was sick, lonely and desperate. I'm so sorry, Lee.

"Two weeks after that, the oncologist put me in the hospital for some tests, and my diagnosis was confirmed. I was devastated. Hearing your voice every night was so comforting. After I got C. J. in bed, I tuned in to WBT and listened for you. Your voice came into my room, and it was as though you were right there with me. I meant to stop. I'm sorry."

Lee cried, "Surely they can operate, they can remove it, can't they, Eddy?"

"They can operate, but the odds aren't good."

"You must try. You have to try".

"I'm a mess, Lee. I can't seem to make decisions. I don't know what to do about C. J.

He has no one. My family disowned me when I married an African American woman. They don't even know about my son, and they'd have nothing to do with him if they did."

"He has me," Lee insisted. "And you have me."

Two weeks before the surgery, Lee moved in with Eddy and C.J. and established a calming routine for the three of them.

On the day of the surgery, she explained everything to the little boy and sent him off to school, instructing him to come to the florist after school as usual, where she would pick him up at closing time.

At the hospital, Lee fought back tears when she saw that Eddy's beautiful hair and pony tail had been shaved. The doctors had marked the left side of his head, where the tumor was located. He was sedated when they transferred him to the gurney that would take him to the operating room, but she knew he could still hear her.

"It's going to be okay Eddy, I'll be right here when you come back."

Three hours later, the surgeon emerged through swinging doors into the waiting room, where she had spent the scariest time of her life.

"We're pretty confident there was no malignancy, but we can't be sure until the lab tests come back," he said. "We'll know tomorrow. Eddy will be in recovery for a while yet, then he'll be heavily sedated for the rest of the day and during the night."

He opened his eyes at 7AM and felt Lee's kiss on his cheek. He saw the sweet smile on her lips. She was holding his hand when the doctor made morning rounds and told him the lab tests came back negative--- no malignant cells. And in a few days, he could go home to a normal life.

Things did get back to normal, well pretty much anyway, except they began planning an amazing wedding. It was to be in their own back yard, and since Eddy was the florist, with every kind of flower imaginable at his disposal, Lee knew they would have the most beautiful wedding ever.

They rented a tent and chairs and hired a band. The caterer brought a three tiered wedding cake topped with a tiny bride and groom. Lee's hair was swept up into a French twist, beneath a short veil that covered her face, and her dress featured a flattering empire waist line. Her special nosegay: white roses, lily of the valley and white azaleas.

The band played *Here Comes the Bride,* while Eddy and C. J. held hands, watching nervously as Lee slowly walked down a rose petal strewn path to join them at the altar, where they became a family.

Afterwards following, Eddy's instructions the band played: *when spring's in the air with its freshness so rare, we'll make our dreams come true.*

## Art in the Park

I backed my station wagon up to the designated unloading zone, grateful I had arrived ahead of the crowd. The registration table lay dead ahead, so I quickly registered and got my booth assignment, which turned out to be on the far side of the park. I had a ways to walk with my paintings, and it was much cooler in Blowing Rock than Clifton, so I was glad I'd brought my sweater.

My landscapes were unframed and not exceptionally large, but it took several trips to get them to my space. This was the third summer I had participated, so I looked forward to seeing familiar faces.

The town had a festive feel, with tourists and summer residents parading up and down the sidewalk, going in and out of shops and licking ice cream cones from the kiosk across the street

Getting a vacation from my hometown of Clifton was a relief. Sometimes I thought of moving away for good, escaping the bad memories. I still lived in the house that held so many, and every gossip in town knew my story:

*** 

Jerry and I met in the tenth grade. We were sweethearts right up until we married, soon after college. Then I started teaching, and he got a job managing Clifton Men's Clothing Store--- perfect for a man who loved to look like he just stepped off a page from the latest Esquire magazine.

Soon every man of any importance came to him to be outfitted, and Jerry Marshall was a born salesman. He had charm, and his main goal in life was to be seen in the right place with the right people. He lived in the glow of his own greatness, but greatness has a short shelf life.

Marriage was nothing like I expected. It seemed our relationship changed overnight. Jerry became cranky, moody, distant, critical and terribly self-indulgent. I wanted to please him, to be the perfect wife, but nothing I did was right. When he complained, I said, "I'm doing my best."

"Your best isn't good enough," he told me.

If I asked for his help with anything, he said, "Your problems are as big as a gnat on an elephant's butt, and I have better things to do."

I taught for a couple of years before I got pregnant with our first child, then two years later, another baby came along. My husband was not interested in his family. He only cared about the men he *dressed for success*. These were the men who invited him to golf at the country club, car races, football games, and fishing trips. He was all about winning friends and influencing people, and he knew how to do it.

After twenty years of marriage, he informed me he was divorcing me to marry a local socialite, the widow of a prominent banker. And although I was shocked, deep down I knew he had been living a secret life. He was moving up in the world, into his girlfriend's fancy brick colonial home on Country Club Drive.

***

But that was then, and today was a wonderful day to be in the mountains. As the art show progressed, my landscape of Grandfather Mountain, with a cluster of

Queen Ann's lace in the foreground, attracted a lot of interest. Eventually a couple from Tennessee bought it for their mountain cabin.

After that success, I decided to take a break, treat myself to a cup of coffee, and sit on one of the park benches facing Main Street. The benches were all occupied, except for one where a man sat alone. I asked if I could share the bench with him.

"Yes, of course," he said, as he continued to stare at the passing traffic.

***

Jerry had been married to Cindy for five years, when one Sunday the headlines in the local paper read:

*LOCAL DOCTOR KILLED IN FIRE. Dr. Robert Hartman was killed in a condo fire in Murells Inlet, South Carolina. Dr. Hartman died in a local hospital. His companion, Jerry Marshall, is being treated at the Chapel Hill Burn Center. When firemen arrived, they found the two men trapped in the bedroom. The fire is believed to have been started by an overturned candle.*

*An official with the Home Owners Association said, "They were a real nice couple who kept to themselves." Hartman and Marshall had owned the condo together for twenty five years.*

***

Later in the afternoon, I was chatting with browsers looking at my artwork, when my park bench partner passed by. He recognized me and offered a polite "Hello."

I sold two more paintings by 6:00 PM, covered my booth with canvas, and left it for park security to guard overnight. I picked up a box dinner and went to my room at the Hemlock Motel for an evening of TV.

Art in the Park didn't open until 10:00 AM on Sunday morning, so I had time for a leisurely breakfast at the Blowing Rock Café. I waited in line for a few minutes before spotting my park bench partner, who motioned for me to share his booth.

I slid into the red leather seat opposite him. "Thanks. I'm Joan Marshall, by the way..."

"Nice to meet you, Joan. I'm Ronald Kincaid. How did the show go for you yesterday?"

"I sold three paintings, not bad for one day. If I do that well today, the show will have been worthwhile. Then I'll spend a few days painting Plein Aire around the mountains and take a few photos before I head home." "Where is home?" he asked.

"Clifton. Where are you from?"

"Raleigh."

The waiter brought my coffee and took my order.

I noticed that Ronald had beautiful white hair, a handsome face, a sensuous mouth and mirthless gray eyes, flecked with bronze. He had a nervous habit of running his fingers through his hair.

When he finished eating, he said, "I'll stop by your booth this afternoon and see how you're doing. Good Luck!"

As I lingered over a second cup of coffee, I wondered what Ronald Kincaid's story was. I had detected something sad behind those eyes, or was he just moody and cranky, like Jerry?

*** 

Being divorced from Jerry Marshall was the best thing that ever happened to me. He wasn't worth the sugar I put in my coffee, and I guess Cindy felt the same way. She couldn't get to her attorney's office fast enough, once she learned the truth about him and Robert. Jerry had been disabled in the fire, and Cindy wasted no time putting him in a nursing home, where he'll spend the rest of his life.

*** 

I paid for my breakfast and headed to the park. Several people from Clifton visited my booth, and I renewed my acquaintance with some of the other exhibitors. Three more paintings sold, and just as I was packing to leave, Ronald appeared.

"Would you like to join me for dinner at the Village Restaurant? I'm not very good company these days, but it would be nice to share a meal with someone."

"I'd love to, but I need to go to the motel and shower first. Could I meet there in about an hour?"

I put on a turquoise silk blouse with a pair of white slacks and walked up the street to the restaurant, where I found Ronald sitting outside at a little café table, drinking wine.

"I'm sorry, I didn't ask you if you were here alone," he apologized. "I am not thinking rationally these days."

"I am alone, and I'm delighted to have someone to keep me company tonight. I sold six paintings this weekend, so I'm in the mood to celebrate."

"Congratulations! Would you like to start with a glass of wine?"

Our table was on the patio under trees strung with little white lights. The spot was so pleasant, we decided to stay outside for our meal. Ronald ordered a whole bottle of wine, and gradually his mood began to lighten.

But I was still wondered what was behind his sad eyes. Would he tell me, "I have cancer, and I have only have a few months to live---or my wife died recently, we had a perfect marriage, and I'm so lonely--- or my wife filed for divorce, and she got the house and half of everything I own--- or my wife has Alzheimer's and she's in a nursing home?"

In light of my past experience, I'm inclined to expect the worst. But I was also thinking, *if you are lonely and looking for a woman, you have rung the wrong bell. I am perfectly content the way I am.*

We had a pleasant dinner in spite of all my negative speculation, and as I was leaving to walk back to the Hemlock Motel, Ronald said, "Would you like to go with me to see the play at the Blowing Rock Theatre tomorrow night?"

We agreed to meet across the street from the theatre at the Mountain Laurel Inn for dinner. By the time I arrived, he had already gotten a table and ordered wine. He seemed more relaxed, dressed in a colorful plaid Ralph Lauren shirt, khaki pants, and handsome
Italian loafers.

Fortunately, the play was a comedy. I laughed a lot, and Ronald let his hair down a little. The cool mountain air was so refreshing when we left the theatre, we decided to stop at a little sidewalk café for a nightcap.

But I was still wondering what was behind his sad eyes. My curiosity was getting the better of me, so I decided to be nosy. "Have you been coming to Blowing Rock long?"

"No, I'm here on business."

A long silence followed. He wiped at the corner of his eye, brushed at his hair, and the sad look returned.

"I just lost my only child," he confessed. "She and her husband were killed in an automobile accident."

"I am so sorry!"

He was quiet for a minute, trying to compose himself. "I buried them a month ago. They owned a summer home here. Their son, my only grandchild, had died in Iraq right after Bush invaded the country. Turns out, I am their only heir.

"You never expect to find yourself in this kind of situation. But you just never know, do you? You try to plan for your future, but you can't plan for something like this. You can buy insurance for almost everything except a broken heart.

"So I came here to check on their house and decide what to do with it. One day, I

93

think I'll sell it--- and the next day, I think I might move here.

"My daughter and her family lived right down the street from me in Raleigh. Every time I drive down that street, it rips my heart out, so I put the Raleigh house on the market. I am not sure I can live there anymore, and
I'm not sure I can live here, either. Everywhere I look, I see things that bring back painful memories."

***

On my way back down the mountain, after leaving Blowing Rock, I thought how good it would be to get home. And I also thought about Ronald and his broken heart. They say time heals all wounds, but it does not. Time simply changes who you are. Eventually, if you're lucky, you learn to find joy in simple things--- like the beauty in your own backyard.

I unloaded the car and went out on my patio. Birds were coming to the feeder for their evening meal. I sat in quiet solitude and watched Mother Nature take her pallet of magnificent peach, pink and gold colors and brush them across the sky.

## Happy Hour at High Peak

You could set your watch by it: 4:30 PM and the ker-plunk, ker-plunk, ker-plunk would be Juliette's walker coming down the sidewalk past a row of duplexes – one cautious step at a time, her feet secured in beige oxfords laced over support hose. She had waited all day for happy hour at the church- run retirement home in High Peak, North Carolina.

Juliette, the widow of a prominent High Peak banker, and Isabella, a retired teacher from a rural area, seemed like unlikely companions.

Juliette lived in a room in the main building, while Isabella lived in a duplex that faced the quadrangle. The duplex had a screened porch, two rocking chairs, and a table holding a pitcher of ice cold *orange blossoms,* made from vodka and orange juice. The drink was Juliette's favorite. A dish of cheese, crackers, and a jar of green pepper jelly were also available for munching.

Juliette breathed heavily as she let the screen door slam behind her and lowered herself into a chair.

Isabella, a frail little lady with snowy hair and a hump on her back, smelled of the Ponds powder she had patted on her face and the White Shoulders perfume she had dabbed behind each ear. Her bright red lipstick bled into the creases around her mouth.

The orange blossoms and the gentle back and forth of the rockers made the world grow soft and mellow. From where they sat, they could watch the sun set over High Peak and their neighbors settling into their usual happy hour routine before heading to the dining room for the evening meal.

"Here comes Esther. She's going to Mary Bess's for sherry," Isabella said. "You know Esther divorced her husband because he had an affair with his secretary. She got the house and a lot of alimony, and she's lived in the lap of luxury ever since."

"Well, he got what he deserved," said Juliette as her gnarled hand brushed at a fly buzzing around her face.

Isabella got up and shooed the fly out the door just as her neighbor, Helena, pulled into the parking space in front of her duplex and entered her front door.

"Would you look at that? Wears nothing but black! And look at those high heeled shoes. Makes my arches throb just looking at them. I don't know how she keeps from breaking her neck in those things," said Isabella.

"Well, she's going to ruin her feet," Juliette said,

"Guess Claude likes black," said Isabella. "Speak of the devil, here he comes!"

Claude, a resident from the opposite side of the quadrangle, pulled his Cadillac in beside Helena's blue Ford and entered her duplex.

"He's come to get his gin and tonic," chuckled Isabella.

Juliette laughed. "That's not the only tonic he gets."

"Helena owned a dress shop downtown. Always looked like a fashion model. Still does, for that matter. She's a lot of fun. Men really like her," said Juliette. "You know, she was shacked up in a hotel room with a High

Peak preacher when he had a heart attack and died in bed with her. People still talk about that. They don't call her the *black widow* for nothing."

"She's a pretty woman, though," said Isabella. "Keeps her figure and wears her shoulder length white hair in a pageboy. And those slenderizing, high- breasted black dresses would turn any man's head."

"Your hair looks nice. Just get it done?"

"Yesterday." Isabella smiled at the compliment. "Put a net on it at night, and it stays pretty good 'til the next week."

"Here, let me pour you another drink," Isabella offered. "And have some more crackers."

Juliette sipped her fresh drink and rocked back and forth. She was sitting on the tiled patio, beside Isabella's potted snake plant, which had tall variegated spikes. "That thing is ugly. You need to throw it out."

"But I've had it for years", said Isabella. "And I don't think it's ugly."

Unable to convince her, Juliette turned her attention back to the street:

"There goes Mrs. Birdsal on her afternoon walk, round and round the quadrangle. Makes me dizzy just watching her. Wears that same old faded dress every day. When she goes into a dress shop, she probably asks them to show her something dowdy. Somebody ought to grab her and wash that dress. And her hair, too, while they're at it. She'll come to dinner with that same old thing on every night.

"Mrs. Birdsal puts a lot of energy into trying to stay healthy and live longer. Lord, I don't know what she's saving herself for. She doesn't understand that none of us are put on this earth to live forever. She'd probably last longer if she'd stop that exercise foolishness and have a little fun, like the rest of us. I'll bet there's not a drop of alcohol to drink in her house." Juliette laughed.

The sun cast shadows across Isabella's porch as Lucy, Isabella's neighbor in the adjoining duplex, came out to water her ferns before heading to the dining room.

"Oh, Lord, be quiet," warned Isabella. "Maybe she won't see us sittin' here drinking. Lucy spent her whole life as a missionary in China saving souls, and now she's got a sinner livin' right next door. That woman could walk across the Yadkin River without getting her feet wet."

"She probably spent all afternoon baking cookies for shut- in's, or making sandwiches for the homeless, after which she treated herself to some nice hot tea in a dainty little tea cup she brought over from China. The closest she's ever been to a man was her preacher, or sitting next to some fellow in a prayer meetin'. What a waste!" Juliette giggled.

"Oh look, here comes Dr. Christenberry on his way to dinner. Now he's a nice man, and good looking too. Taught Biology at NC State, you know. Would have been a good catch for somebody, and plenty of women were all over him when he first moved in. But he let them know right away he wasn't interested. I hear he's a wonderful Bridge player, travels all over the state to play in tournaments," Isabella finished.

And they both watched in silence until the handsome Dr. Christenberry was out of sight

Juliette sighed. "Well, I guess you heard about Liz Robertson?"

"No, what about her?"

"She fell in the dining room last night and broke her hip. Florence was helping her to her table. She saw her falling, but couldn't get to her in time. Liz is in the hospital now, but they're bringing her back here to Health Care tomorrow."

"Have you met Elizabeth Thornton yet?" asked Isabella. "She just moved in last week. Taught art at Woman's College, and she never married. Real peculiar, hard to talk to. Artist are strange people anyway, don't you think?

Isabella said, "Tomorrow is Sunday. Wish I could go to church, but I can't see or hear well enough anymore. The new preacher comes to visit me, though. He's nice enough, but he has a beard. What decent preacher would wear a beard? Guess I'll go to vespers up in the main building. Dr. Rogers is preaching on the book of Job.

"Well, Job is so depressing." Juliette frowned. "The last thing I want to do is sit and listen to a sermon on boils."

Juliette said. "My daughter always comes on Sunday afternoon, and she's bringing me some deviled eggs. They don't make deviled eggs in retirement homes, and Lord how I miss 'em. Tomorrow I think I'll just go sit on the sun porch and listen to a book on tape until my daughter gets here."

"Speaking of food, guess it's about time to go to dinner. I want to get back here in time to watch Lawrence Welk on TV," said Isabella.

"How can you watch that irritating man? His wunnerful, wunnerful little champagne bubbles get on my nerves." Juliette scowled and got serious. "Now I want you to promise me something, Isabella..."

"What?"

"If you ever come to my room and find me lying there dead, take all the vodka bottles from under my bed and get rid of them before you ring for the nurse."

"If that ever happens, I surely will." Isabella laughed. "But right now, all I can think about is dinner. Lets' go. Here, let me help you up."

# The Bus Stop

I got off the bus and walked down a desolate, snowy street under a gray sky to the Mercy Nursing Home in Charlotte, North Carolina. It had been two months since I moved to the sunny south, and I swear, I could count on one hand the days I'd seen any sun.

It snowed two days ago, and after the first flake these crazy people started racing to the grocery store buying bread and milk.

As I approached the nursing home, a man wearing several layers of clothes and a knitted cap was pouring salt on the steps. He took my elbow.

"Let me help you, ma'am, watch your step." Suddenly his hand tightened on my elbow so much it hurt.

"Indiana, what in world?" he said "You ain't got no business being out here in the cold. Have you lost your mind? If you gonna wander off like this, they'll tie you to a chair."      "I'm not Indiana," I told him.

He was pulling me toward the door when I said, "Stop! I told you, I'm not Indiana, I'm Missouri, her sister. Now take your hands off me."

I walked through the front door, leaving him shaking his head and mumbling to himself.

The young girl at the desk was so busy shuffling through some papers, she didn't bother to look up. I said. "Can you tell me what room Indiana Smith is in?"

"Go down the hall and turn left at the end. Then it's the first door on the left, room 230."

I passed by a lot of silver haired people sitting around in wheelchairs. Some were staring into space and drooling all over themselves.

One of them yelled, "Hey lady, come over here. I got somethin' to tell you."

One grabbed my hand and said, "Will you get me some juice?"

The smell of urine made my eyes water. I passed a laundry cart filled with dirty smelling clothes, and next to it, a nurse at a medicine cart was pouring pills into little paper cups.

The door to room 230 was open, so I walked right in. Her back was to me as she sat by the window. And when she turned around, I thought I was looking at my own self in a mirror. Our wiry hair had turned white and our faces were full of wrinkles. My sister was wearing pink, her favorite color that I never cared much for.

She looked at me with a blank stare. "Hey, Indiana, I'm your sister Missouri," I said.

My heart was beatin' so fast and I was shaking so bad I could hardly get my breath. I felt my legs 'bout to give way, so I sat down on the side of her bed.

In a few minutes her eyes lit up and she gave me her proud smile, showing off her two front teeth with the little space between them- just like mine and our mama's.

***

Our great-great-great grandfather came from Charlotte. His name was Matthew McCorkle, the name his slave master gave him. After the emancipation, he left North Carolina for a better life.

And you are probably wondering how I got here. Well, it wasn't no easy road, I tell you.

105

Only through the grace of Lord Jesus Christ, am I here today.

James McCorkle married Loretta Moore, my mother. Truth be told, they shouldn't 'a ever got married. They didn't even like each other. She got pregnant not long after they married and had twin girls, in a little shack with a neighbor woman helping her birth 'em.

When it come time to name us, since we lived on the line between two states, she named me Missouri and my sister Indiana.

James McCorkle was a mean man. He would come home drunk and beat our mama. My earliest memories were her beggin' him to stop. Me and Indiana got so scared, we'd hide under the house with our arms around each other.

Daddy had a brother named Robert, and he was about the best looking black man you ever laid eyes on. Well, that's what I thought anyway, and I guess Mama thought so, too. Because one day she and Robert flew the coop for parts unknown.

She left a note on the kitchen table for daddy: "We can only take one girl, so you take care of the other one."

I was the other one.

I stayed mad at Mama for years. Actually, I still am. How could she go off and leave me?

I dreamed every night she'd come back and get me. I really believed she would. I prayed and I cried for years--- for her and for my twin sister.

My daddy had one woman after another living with us. They were just as mean as he was, and not one of them had the sense God gave a goose. Bessie was the last one. I just pure-T couldn't stand her. She would send me down the road to the gas station to buy her cigarettes and beer.

A boy named Danny Ford worked at the gas station. He would flirt with me, and I admit, I gave him my sweetest smile--- flashing my pearly whites between my ruby red lips. He would kinda rubbed up against me a little. I was so starved for attention, I just let him rub, and then we ended up in the woods behind the gas station, and well--- you can figure out the rest.

Danny played the guitar and thought he could make a living playing with a band. He was twenty- five and I was sixteen when he asked me to go with him to Branson. I didn't have no better place to be, so I went.

The only thing Danny managed to do in Branson was get me pregnant. He was the first of the four men who did. And I never married a one of them. Not one of them was worth the sugar I put in my tea. They were all piddley- ass losers. But I had faith that God would look after me. Sure wadn't nobody else gonna do it.

I raised all four of my children by working for white people. My kids all graduated from high school and got good jobs. Now, they don't have no time for me, and I got grandchildren I don't even know.

I thought I would live out the rest of my life in my little house, going to the Seventh Day Adventist Church, knowing that God would take care of me. I tried to forgive my mama and accept that I would never see my beloved sister again.

The only one of my children who remembered my seventieth birthday was my daughter, Charity, who lives in Charlotte. Well don't you know, God does work in mysterious ways. Charity come for me with a U-Haul, and before I knew it, I was on my way to North Carolina.

Charity is divorced and has one child, Latisha, who I had never even seen. She's a real sweet girl, and we get along just fine. She don't talk much, 'cause like everybody else, she sits around with a device of one kind or another in her hand. If it ain't her laptop, it's her IPod--- or she's texting, god knows who, on her cell phone.

If she has a boyfriend, I ain't heard nothin' about him. She's a little on the heavy side. That comes from sittin' on the sofa eating potato chips and Oreos. Latisha sure aint' like me when I was sixteen. I was burning up calories in the woods behind the gas station with Danny Ford.

One day Latisha asked me didn't I have no other family besides her and her mama? I explained about Mama leavin' me and takin' my twin sister instead. I told her how I spent my whole life wondering where Indiana was and thinking how I would love to see her again before I die.

Charity said to me, "Mama, there's got to be a way to find your sister, and I'm going to get on *Ancestry.com* and see if I can do it. I'll put in where you were born and your birthday, and see what comes up..."

She started working on her laptop, and in a little while she said, "Come look, Mama, I found you and Indiana in a census. I put in Loretta Moore McCorkle, and can you believe this – I found her death certificate, and she died right here in Charlotte! Now if I can find an obituary, it'll tell us about her survivors."

Charity didn't find no obituary, but she found where she was buried on *FindAGrave.com.* Turned out Mama was buried at Mariah Baptist Church, right here in Charlotte.

Next Charity called the church and asked about Loretta's survivors. She got the names of five children, and one of them was Indiana. Another was a son who lived close by.

"He still goes to church here, and I have his telephone number."

Charity dialed the number, and when a man answered, she told him her mama was looking for her sister, Indiana.

He said, "Indiana's right here in Charlotte, in the Mercy Nursing Home. And you can tell Missouri she's got some half brothers and sisters and more nieces and nephews than you can shake a stick at. Thank God for bringing her to us. One of these days we gonna have us one big old family reunion."

\*\*\*

So now, I sat on Indiana's bed, almost too overcome to talk, until she held out her arms to me, and I walked over and hugged her.

I soon found out there wasn't nothing wrong with her mind. She remembered everything about our childhood and how she and Mama left me behind with our good- for- nothin' daddy. We talked endlessly for hours, until the man from the icy steps stuck his head in the door.

"This is Gabe," Indiana told me.

"Yeah, we met before," Gabe said. "And I'm awful sorry, but you took me by surprise. You see, Indiana is my sister-in-law, but I didn't know nothin' about you….

"I'll be leaving soon, and I thought maybe you'd let me give you a ride home, Missouri, so you won't have to stand out in the cold waiting for the bus."

Me and Gabe walked across the parking lot to his car, and this time, I was real glad when he took my elbow to help me across the icy spots.

After that, I went to the nursing home every Wednesday to hear about the half brothers and sisters I never knew I had.

Gabe made a habit of finding some kind of yard work to do in front of the building, so he could say hello when I got off the bus. And he always came to my sister's room to drive me home in the afternoon.

On our rides home, we got to know each other. Gabe had been in love with a woman who lived with him for ten years, until she ran off with a roofer, who was working on the house next door. I told him how Mama ran off with Uncle Robert, who also lived next door, and how she left me behind.

"Missouri, your Mama had to be plumb crazy to go off and leave you. And I can tell you, your uncle Robert and Indiana didn't have no easy time living with that woman. But at least you got your sister back, and you got people here that love you."

Gabe had a way of making me feel better, and he made me realize that everybody has a cross to bear. He said I was smart and brave. Nobody had ever been that nice before.

One afternoon, he asked me to come home with him, and said he would cook my supper. When I told him how much I liked his southern cooking, he said if I liked it so much, why didn't I move in with him?

Gabe retired from the nursing home, and now he works most days in his garden. He still cooks a lot, because he likes to please me. And there ain't nothin' in this world I wouldn't do for that man. We may be up in years, but we get along just fine.

When I think of all the crap I had to put up with to finally get a few years of happiness, I say,

"Thank you Jesus!"

# Night Terrors

My body stiffened, I jumped straight up screaming. I was so hot my pajamas and sheets were sweaty and twisted in knots. I wanted to run, but run from what? Waves of dizziness swept over me as I staggered to the bathroom, got a drink of water and sat in the dark trying to calm down.

\*\*\*

As far back as I can remember, I have awakened in the night screaming and my grandfather used to come running into my room, pick me up, and kiss my cheek saying, "It's okay honey, don't be afraid. Papa's got you now." And he would rock me until I fell asleep again.

I went to live with my grandparents when I was three years old. I loved Papa so much and Granny, too, but she was not as patient, especially when I had nightmares. But she did do nice things, like bake cookies and make pretty clothes for me.

Carol, my mother, was their only child. She was a *daddy's girl,* and after she died, I was all they had left. Papa doted on me. Granny said he spoiled me, and she lived by the old proverb: *spare the rod and spoil the child.*

My grandmother, Myrtle Beam was the daughter of a Baptist Preacher, Clyde Beam. He had two churches where he preached every other Sunday. In between, he farmed some rocky, hilly land outside Waynesville.

We made regular visits to the Beam's old home place. That family had all died, except Granny's brother, Richard, who worked a prosperous apple orchard on the family farm land. Uncle Richard always sent us home with a bushel basket of golden delicious apples, wrapped in little purple tissue papers, which Papa carried down to the cellar where they stayed nice and crisp for months.

Papa, Granny, and I went to Holy Gospel Baptist Church every Sunday, where I had a nearly perfect Sunday school attendance record. Each Sunday I got to place a gold star on a chart beside my name.

Granny made me read a chapter in the Bible every night before my prayers. She placed a little rug by my bed that she had braided from colorful scraps of cloth saved from making my dresses. I had to kneel on the little rug and say: "*Now I lay me down to sleep, I pray the Lord my soul to keep. If I should die before I wake, I pray the Lord my soul to take.*"

After Granny turned out the light, I had a prayer of my own--- just between me and God, asking Him to please help me be a good girl and make the nightmares stop.

My nightmares upset Papa and Granny a lot. I heard them talking, and I knew Granny thought I was possessed by the devil. Sometimes in my nightmare, it felt like I really was burning in hell. I worried myself sick trying to imagine what terrible thing I could have done to cause God to punish me that way.

Papa would say to Granny, "Myrtle, you know very well why that poor child has them nightmares, and you need to stop with that devil talk. You got them crazy notions from that Bible thumping daddy of yours."

They had a picture of Mama in her wedding dress on the mantle above the fireplace, right next to the picture of Jesus and the gold cross with the words *Jesus Saves* written across it. Granny told me my mama was in heaven with Jesus, but they never mentioned my daddy.

They told me that Mama and Daddy died in an automobile accident when I was three years old. I don't remember my parents at all. Papa would say, "You sure do remind me of your mama, child, you got her strawberry blonde hair and her sweet smile."

My mama is buried in Waynesville. Granny bought plastic flowers at K-mart to put on her grave at Easter and Christmas. I asked why we didn't take flowers to Daddy, but they said it was because they didn't know where he was buried.

Except for the nightmares, I had a pretty nice childhood. I made good grades. Granny taught me to sew, and I loved going to town to buy new patterns and pretty cloth from Belk. I also loved to read, and got two or three library books every week.

Granny didn't approve of parties, dances or playing cards. She absolutely disapproved of me going out with boys. I always felt different because the other kids had real parents, not old grandparents like me.

I worried sometimes that maybe I had something to do with my parent's automobile accident. I asked a lot of questions that went unanswered---questions about my father and my paternal grandparents. Why couldn't I visit them? Maybe they didn't like me because of the bad thing I must have done.

When I got too big for Papa to rock me at night, he still came into my room when he heard my screams. He sat on the bed and held my hand until I calmed down.

One night, Papa didn't come in to supper at his usual time, and Granny sent me out to the barn to see about him. I found him on the ground right outside the tool shed. He'd had a heart attack. The person I loved more than anything in the world was gone.

Granny was as lost as I was without him. She depended on me for everything, and I took care of her until she died.

***

I sat by the window and watched the moonbeams dance across my floor until I felt peaceful enough to go back to bed. After all, I had to be at my job at the library at 8:00 in the morning.

Sometimes I thought I was going stark raving mad, and eventually I made an appointment at the local mental health clinic. I was a nervous wreck when I walked into the psychiatrist's office. The doctor, who asked me to call him Jeff, shook my hand and directed me to sit on a soft chair across from him.

"I understand from the forms you filled out that you are having night terrors."

"Yes," I said.

"Pease start as far back as you can remember, and describe them to me."

I was embarrassed. I didn't want him to know what a sorry, sad person I had become.

"Our first session is mostly for me to get to know you, to get a feel for what we have to work on here. I'd like you to keep a diary of your nightmares. Write down what happened that day how you felt when you went to bed, then come see me in a week."

The next week, I took my diary to the appointment. I'd had three nightmares that week. When Jeff asked me about my grandparents, I told him everything.

After that, I found myself looking forward to my sessions. I didn't especially want to talk about my problems, I wanted to see Jeff. He was warm, kind, and caring.

After about six weeks, I couldn't get Jeff out of my mind. My inappropriate attraction to him had to stop. I needed to end the sessions, so I made some excuses and told him I wouldn't be back.

The very next week, Jeff showed up at the library where I worked. My heart skipped a beat when he walked up to the desk.

"Hello, Amy," he said. "Now that you aren't my patient anymore, I am free to ask you to have coffee with me when you get off." "Thanks, Jeff. I'm sorry, but I can't. I have to work late."

"No problem, I'll wait. I'll read one of these books until you get off."

So I couldn't get out of it.

After making him wait a decent interval, we went to the little café across the street and ordered coffee. I was nervous and even more nervous when he said:

"I worry about something you mentioned in one of our sessions---that thing about being punished. God doesn't punish people, and
certainly not little children."

Next Jeff wrote something on a pad and handed it to me: *This I know for sure, Amy, you are not a bad person, and you are not being punished. Jeff McDonald--- 302-8565.*

He pushed it across the table and said, "Put this beside your bed, and every time you have a nightmare, read it, and then call me."

Then he paused and looked into my eyes.

"You know what, Amy? I'm glad you ended the sessions, because I'd like to spend some time just having fun with you. I don't think you've had much joy in your life, and I'd to change that."

119

That night he talked me into ordering dinner, and then going to a movie. I did have fun, but having fun frightened me, and so did being with Jeff.

After that, once every week, when I was busy checking out books to patrons, I would look up and see him in line. He would hand me a note written on his little pad, asking me to meet him at the café when I got off.

One day I accessed *Ancestry.com* on the library computers and decided it would be fun to look up my family. I started on my lunch break with the easiest part first, which was Granny's family.

I typed in "Myrtle Jean Beam, born Waynesville, North Carolina, May 5, 1900, father, Clyde Monroe Beam--- mother, Ethel Louise Stark--- spouse, James Allen Taylor--- child, Carol Ann Taylor."

Eventually, I went to *Find a Grave* and discovered a picture of Mama's grave in the cemetery in Waynesville.

Holding my breath, I entered my daddy's name: "Jimmy Dean Dellinger--- born November 13, 1920, Hendersonville, North Carolina."

His name appeared on my screen, but when I went to *Find a Grave,* I got no result. When I looked for Daddy's death certificate, nothing came up. Next I checked obituaries in the 1923 local papers. Nothing.

But an article in the Waynesville paper popped up:

*September 12, 1923.*

*DAUGHTER OF LOCAL FAMILY MURDERED. Neighbors rescued a three year old child from a burning home early this morning. The child, identified as Amy Lynn Dellinger, is recovering in a local hospital from burns she received in the fire. The body of Carol Ann Taylor Dellinger, with multiple stab wounds, was discovered inside the burning building. Police are searching for Jimmy Dean Dellinger, for questioning concerning the death of his wife.*

I just made it to the bathroom, before I threw up.

I broke out in a cold sweat. I couldn't stop shaking. My brain raced with visions of flames and sirens and a baby screaming. And then I rubbed my fingers across the little scars on my arms and legs that had never completely faded away--- the scars Papa and Granny would never talk about.

I leaned against the back of the commode until my body to stop jerking.

When I was able to speak, I left the bathroom and told my supervisor I was coming down with flu and had to go home.

I walked into my apartment, opened a bottle of wine, poured myself a glass, and tried to think. I turned on my computer, found *Ancestry.com,* clicked on membership, typed in my credit card, and finally I was in business.

I needed to know everything. I pulled up the newspaper again and typed in *September 13, 1923:*

*Jimmy Dean Dellinger was captured late yesterday and charged with the murder of his wife, Carol Ann Taylor Dellinger and the attempted murder of his infant daughter Amy Lynn Dellinger, who is recovering from burns in a local hospital.*

I kept looking at newspaper articles until I found June 1924:

*Jimmy Dean Dellinger was tried and convicted of the murder of his wife Carol Ann Dellinger and the attempted murder of his daughter, Amy Lynn Dellinger. He was sentenced to life in prison and transported to a maximum security prison in Tennessee.*

The monster was still alive!

I was too numb to think. I just sat and stared out the window for a long time, trying to put together the pieces of this horrible puzzle. It was beginning to get dark when the doorbell rang.

"I stopped by the library and learned you had come down with flu," Jeff said. "I brought some chicken soup from the café.

God, you do look sick, Amy, maybe you should see a doctor?"

"I'm not sick," I said.

"I don't understand."

"But I found this on Ancestry.com..." I pulled up the first newspaper article. "Please read this."

Jeff said nothing as he absorbed the words on the screen. My heart kept time with the ticking of the wall clock as I watched the crease between his eyes deepen and his face turn red. Finally, he pushed back from the computer.

"My god, the bastard!" he muttered through clenched teeth.

He grabbed me and held me tight while I sobbed uncontrollably.

"Amy, I am so sorry."

Neither of us said anything for a long time. He caressed the scars on my arms and gently kissed me.

"I'm so ashamed," I confessed. "It's horrible to think that my own father did this to my mother and me, and that I carry his genes!"

"His bad behavior doesn't make you a bad person, and now that you've uncovered the secret of your past, you're free to plan your future. Believe me, Amy, you deserve a future filled with love and happiness."

"Jeff, I'm still trying to come to grips with all this. Can you stay for a while? I don't want to be alone."

"I am not going anywhere, Amy."

## Love Grows in a Red, Red Rose

It was gone, burned to the ground--- the house and barn--- everything a smoldering pile of ashes.  I had saved and borrowed to own this farm. The horses, cows and sheep ran up into the mountains, and god knew where they were now.  Even if I could find them, I had nowhere to put them and nothing to feed them.

I was sitting on the watering trough, the only thing left, my head in my hands, feeling all hollowed out, when Charlie came cowering out of the woods and licked my face. I put my arms around him and pulled him to me.

News traveled fast, even here in the North Carolina Mountains. It wasn't long before the banker came about the loan I owed on the land that now belonged to him.

The sky was cloudless as the sun rose, and Charlie and I set out walking down the dusty dirt road toward Asheville. I thought about Roxie, the love of my life, who had refused to marry me, choosing instead a man who had more to offer her. My heart still ached from her rejection and now this.

A wagon approached, and when it pulled up beside me, the driver yelled, "Whoa. Mister, you look like you need a ride. Where you headed?"

"Goin' to Asheville. Needin' a job," I said.

"Git in. I know where you can git one. A rich man named Vanderbilt bought 120,000 acres, and he's building the biggest house in the whole country. Goin' there myself. Place will have a farm on it and all kinds of flower gardens. They hirin' anybody willing to work. Name's Johnson."

"I'm Rush Slade," I said, "And thank you for the ride."

Johnson was right about the size of the Vanderbilt place. The house alone covered several acres. They were just starting on the farm land, and I was put to work getting it ready for spring planting. Besides the work being done on the house, people were putting up split rail fence, building lakes, and clearing land for flower gardens. If the work got caught up in one place, you were sent to another area. Charlie and I lived in a one room shack there on the grounds.

People were talking about some famous man coming to do the landscaping. He had designed gardens all over the country. In early September, Frederick Olmstead arrived. Mr. Vanderbilt wanted an English type garden, but Mr. Olmstead refused and located the gardens next to the house, because he wanted a view of the mountains in the background. For days he walked over the land, before setting up an office where he started drawing blueprints of what he wanted done.

When work on the farm land was done, they me sent to help out with landscaping. I learned how to read blueprints, mark off plots-- things I never even dreamed about. I hauled rock and dug thousands of holes. I planted the shipments of tulip, crocus, narcissus, hyacinth, iris and other flowers you didn't usually see in these parts.

Olmstead designed the arboretum to stretch all the way to the French Broad River, and then back to the house. Between it and the house, he planned a rose garden, with plots laid out in different shapes and sizes that fit together like a jig saw puzzle. Each plot was designed to hold a different color rose. We built arches for the climbing roses.

Laurel, rhododendron, boxwoods, azaleas and shrubs of every kind imaginable dotted the gardens. Wisteria- covered arbors, and latticed gazeboes were scattered throughout.

Trucks came up the road bringing all sorts of things. Some of it came from Europe. One day I looked up to see a woman carved in marble riding up the driveway on a truck. They said the statue's name was Diana, goddess of the hunt and moon. Later, a bronze fish was delivered. When we got him set up in the middle of a goldfish pond, water squirted out of his mouth.

From time to time, George Vanderbilt himself showed up to see how things were coming along. He was a fancy dresser, alright. As I watched him stroll around in his nice suit, I thought to myself, someday I'm gonna buy a good suit, a nice hat, and own my own place again. I'll never be like George Vanderbilt, but I don't mean to be a nobody forever. I'll work for him until I've saved enough money to do what I want.

In early spring, bulbs sent shoots out of the ground where frost had been. Tiny flowers raised their faces to the sun. Rose bushes came alive in all their glorious colors. Nothing was as sweet as the perfume a red rose gave off on a hot summer day.

I learned the latest farming techniques and landscaping from Mr. Olmstead himself, who was considered the father of landscaping. But more than anything, I loved growing and tending the beautiful roses.

In December of 1895, Mr. Vanderbilt and his wife and daughter moved into their French Chateau. A huge fir tree was placed beside the stone fireplace in the great hall. I helped carry in hundreds of poinsettias that were placed all around downstairs. On Christmas Eve, they invited hundreds of guests in to help them celebrate.

Sometime after Christmas, I was sent down to the village to pick up some things from a farm store. I signed for the supplies, and when I turned to go, I bumped into a woman.

I said, "I'm sorry." But, I wasn't really.

Her green eyes looked into mine. She smiled at me and said, "That's quite all right." She wore a simple dress, and her straw- colored hair looked as though the wind had gently blown through it, leaving curly strands around her face.

The clerk said, "Miss Chrissy, this is Rush Slade. He works up at The Biltmore House. He might be able to find you some help."

"My name is Chrissy Odom," she told me. "My father died recently and left me the family farm. I need a foreman. Would you come to the farm, so we can talk?"

I must have lost my mind for a minute. I already had a good job, but I said, "Yes ma'am, tell me how to get there."

The long winding road to Miss Chrissy's crossed a mountain stream that rushed under a washed out bridge before continuing on through a canopy of rhododendron and hemlocks. The road led to a large house that had once been white. It had a wrap-around porch beneath a scrolled balcony. On either side of the door were stained glass windows, the kind you see in a church.

I prayed I wouldn't step on a snake as I waded through knee deep weeds to a weathered door. Attached was a shiny brass door knocker, with MARGARET CHRISTINE ODOM engraved on it.

Chrissy Odom welcomed me into the foyer, where sun was shining though the stained glass windows, casting colorful shapes across the pine plank floor. She led me past a mirrored hall tree, where a couple of men's hats hung--- probably her daddy's.

We went into a sitting room filled with musty furniture and a piano. Walnut tables sat on either side of a blue velvet sofa, and over it hung a portrait of Clarence Odom, a prosperous and well- respected farmer in his day.

Miss Chrissy sat on the sofa and motioned for me to join her. Then she explained how she didn't need anybody to tell her how to run her farm. She would do it just like her daddy did. But she needed someone to carry out her instructions and to supervise the farm hands.

She owned a barn, where she kept several horses. She also had a good size herd of cattle, a few dozen sheep, some hogs, and a pen full of chickens.

The most pressing need on the farm was hay and feed for the livestock. And every damn where I looked, I saw things that needed to be done. The place was pitiful. After all, I had been working at The Biltmore House, where I saw what money could buy. I had no business gettin' tangled up with a hardheaded woman, who clearly said she didn't need anybody to tell her how to run her farm. Plus she didn't have two pennies to rub together.

I said, "Well, Miss Odom, I don't think you really need me."

"Oh, Mr. Slade, but I do. I would be willing to give you half of the proceeds, as long as you keep the livestock fed properly and the help busy. You may live in the cabin located back of the big house."

"I'd be bringing a sheep dog with me."
"Oh, I love dogs! We used to have sheep dogs, but I haven't had one since I was a child. When can you come?"

I said, "Miss Chrissy, I can come help, but only for a little while. I have some other things to do."

Soon Charlie and I settled into the little cabin. I met the farm workers, Lester and Benny, who also lived on the property. A girl named Macy had been moved into the big house, when Miss Chrissy learned that she had been being beaten by her stepfather.

I walked all over the farm, checking the fences and figuring out what I needed to do before spring planting. Every piece of machinery needed repairing. The wheels were off the wagons, and the axels were dragging the ground.

Eighty year old Oliver Anderson owned the farm adjoining Miss Chrissy's. He was still farming the same way his daddy did fifty years ago, but Oliver had more up-to-date machinery, which he agreed to let me use if

I would help with his crops and supervise his farm hands.

To my surprise, Miss Chrissy stayed out of my way and let me use the skills I'd learned at Biltmore, which produced the best crops the Odom and Anderson farms had ever seen.

What we didn't keep to feed the animals, we sold at a good price.

We killed hogs, cut enough firewood for everybody to keep warm, and in the spring, we planted a vegetable garden that fed everybody on the place.

With the important work out of the way, I had the farm hands plow the yard around Miss Chrissy's house and plant grass. I was anxious to try my skills at landscaping, so I drew plans for new shrubbery.

In a nice sunny spot beside the house, we dug a place to put a rose garden. We brought cow manure up from the barn to mix with the rich mountain loam. And when I say *we*, I mean Miss Chrissy and me. She loved being outside, getting her hands dirty, and she was real excited about growing her own roses.

I got Clarence Odom's old truck running again, and asked Chrissy if she'd like to go with me down to the Biltmore house to choose some rose bushes. I took her on a tour of the gardens and greenhouses, where my friends let us pick a good number of rose bushes with name tags attached. I told her that she and the Vanderbilt's would have the finest rose gardens in the whole state--- or maybe in the country.

Miss Chrissy worked by my side as we put the roses in the ground. I loved having her close to me, but I kept my emotional distance. I wasn't going to let myself be hurt by another woman. Besides, to her, I was just one of the hired hands.

My dog, Charlie, was a different story. The only distance he had to worry about was the distance he had to run to fetch the ball Chrissy threw for him. She took him in the house and bathed him, brushed him, and she bought him a fancy collar. After a while, he didn't know which one of us he belonged to. He ran back and forth from one house to the other.

Sometimes she would yell down to my cabin, "Rush, don't bother feeding Charlie, he's already eaten."

Miss Chrissy decided she wanted to learn to drive the truck, so I started teaching her to drive around the barnyard. Before I knew it, she was taking off down to the village, the wind blowing her hair out the window, and Charlie sitting up in the seat beside her. She was the most carefree soul I had ever seen, about as happy as a body could be.

One day she came up the driveway with a bird bath in the back of the truck, which she had me place in the rose garden. She also had some wind chimes that she hung from a trellis I'd made for the pink Angel Delight climbing roses.

Then I decided to surprise her and build a gazebo. I built it in Oliver's barn, so she wouldn't know what I was up to. Just before Christmas, Lester, Benny and I loaded it on the truck and put it in the garden. Chrissy was so happy, she was speechless.

Once she regained her composure, she asked me to come inside. She told me how much money we had made, and that all our debts were paid. "My father would be so proud!"

Chrissy was planning a Christmas dinner for the farm hands and their families, to show her appreciation. She asked me to cut a tree for her and Macy to decorate.

"I haven't had a Christmas tree in years," Miss Chrissy said. "There's a box of decorations in the attic, and I'm going to buy new lights and a star for the top. We're going to have a wonderful Christmas, because we have a lot to celebrate."

I got a haircut, had my beard trimmed, and purchased a new suit in the Village. I bought Miss Chrissy a poinsettia and a pretty blue glass vase with gold trim, which I had wrapped in shiny red paper and tied with a white satin ribbon.

A long table covered with a white cloth stretched from one end of the dining room to the other.  Holly and red candles decorated the center. Chrissy and Macy had spent days making fruit cakes and pecan pies. Wonderful aromas circulated all around the house, and Chrissy was taking a turkey out of the oven when I arrived.

I was surprised when she asked me to sit at the head of the table and carve the turkey. Macy, Lester, Benny and their families were seated all around us. She was all smiles as we filled our plates with her good food. Charlie had his own bowl beside the kitchen stove, where he got his share of turkey and gravy.

Chrissy had a box of apples, oranges, nuts and candy for each family, and an envelope with money for me. After the others went home, she asked me to stay while she unwrapped my gift and poured us each a glass of brandy.

Then on New Year's Day, I saw a strange car pull up in front of Chrissy's house.  It came almost every day for a week.  As soon as I got Macy alone, I asked her who it belonged to.

"Oh my lord, that's Mr. Andrew Hamilton, Miss Chrissy's old boyfriend. That man ain't no good. She thought she got shed of him, but here he come again."

Toward the end of January, Chrissy left with Andrew Hamilton, and she didn't come back for a week. When she finally returned, Hamilton came along, with all his clothes in two suitcases.

Late one afternoon, Macy knocked on my door. "Mr. Rush, Miss Chrissy done gone off and married that awful man! He's making me sleep in the cellar, and he says he better not catch that mangy dog of yours in there no more. He say *he* the man around here now, and everybody gotta do what *he* say-- or else."

In the meantime, old Oliver Anderson had been talking to me about buying his farm. He offered me a good deal for the land, the house, and everything that went with it.

Now that Andrew Hamilton had made it known that he was the man in charge, it was time for me to leave Chrissy's place.

I watched Hamilton drive out of the yard one morning, and pretty soon Miss Chrissy came looking for me. She said, "I guess Macy told you I got married."

"Yes," I admitted, as I noticed an ugly bruise on her cheek. "Does that hurt"?

"It's not so bad," she said, refusing to meet my eyes.

"What happened?"

"I tripped and fell," she whispered.

I knew she was lying. "I don't believe that, Chrissy. Please tell me the truth."

Tears were in her eyes as she turned and slowly walked back to the house.

After that, every chance I got, I asked Macy what was going on.

Finally Macy confessed:

"Mr. Hamilton just stays drunk all the time, and he keeps tellin' Miss Chrissy to give him more money. Miss Chrissy tells him that money's meant for the farm, but he don't care. She cries all the time, but he tells her to shut up, or he'll slap her. I'm so scared, Mr.

Rush. I just know somethin' terrible is gonna happen up there."

"You come get me if Chrissy needs help, you hear?" I insisted. "If he ever hits her again, you let me know."

One cold February night, Macy knocked on my door:

"He's real drunk this time, Mr. Rush. They's in the bedroom. Miss Chrissy just keeps on a screaming, and keeps on sayin', *Please don't kill me. I'll give you the money!*

"Then Mr. Hamilton says, *It's too late now. I know a way to get all your money, your farm, and everything you own, bitch!*"

I loaded the pistol I kept under my pillow, ran up to the big house, and quietly opened the door to their bedroom. Andrew Hamilton had his wife on the bed, a pistol to her head.

He was so drunk, he didn't hear me come in, but Chrissy saw me. I motioned for her to slide to one side, and when she did, I called his name. He turned around and pointed his gun at me, so I shot him.

She pushed him off of her as his blood spattered on her dress and all over the sheets.

"Rush!" she screamed, "Thank god you came. He was going to kill me!"

She threw her arms around me, and I could feel her heart pounding against my chest. "He won't hurt you now," I promised.

By then, Macy was standing in the doorway screaming. I told her to run and get Lester and Benny.

We all had to wait a good while for the sheriff to arrive. Chrissy wanted to take off her blood stained clothes, but I told her we best leave everything for the sheriff to see. Otherwise, he might arrest me for murder.

I held her close and tried to keep her calm. She told me how Andrew had sweet talked her into marrying him, how he told her how much he loved her, and that they were meant to be together.

She said, "Rush, marrying him was the stupidest thing I have ever done. My life was so happy until he showed up, lied to me, and made promises he never intended to keep." Luckily, the sheriff believed our story. When he asked Chrissy what she wanted done with the body, she said, "I don't care, just get him far away from me."

Chrissy wouldn't come out of the house after the shooting. I knew she was upset and embarrassed about what had happened and needed time to recover.

Hard as it was, I stayed away. But I kept asking Macy about her. I also told Macy to let Chrissy know I was there, if she needed me. "I done told her, Mr. Rush," Macy said. "But she's too shamed to show her face, especially to you. She says everybody thinks she's a fool, and that's exactly what she is. She say she don't know what on earth *you* must think of her."

Time passed slowly, and every Sunday, I dressed in my good suit and went to the little church down the mountain. Chrissy hadn't been since the shooting. All kinds of wild tales were going around. Some folks even thought Chrissy had gone insane and locked herself in an upstairs room.

Finally, in early June, Margaret Christine Odom entered the church and walked proudly down the red carpeted aisle. Every head turned and stared with curiosity as she slipped in the pew beside me. I knew how hard this was for her. I smiled and squeezed her hand. I had missed her so much.

She told me her rose garden was in full bloom, and I found her there the next week. She looked happy again, back to her old self, as she pruned and cut off dead blooms--- just the way I had taught her.

She laughed as she cut a deep red Mr. Lincoln rose, held it under my nose and said, "Rush, have you ever smelled anything so sweet?"

I was happy, too, and wanted to share my good news. I told her I had bought Oliver's farm and would be leaving her little cabin soon. Much to my surprise, she turned white as a sheet, then turned and ran into the house.

I followed and found her crying on the sofa.

"So, all this time you were planning to leave me!" she sobbed "Is it because I stupidly married Andrew, or have I offended you?"

I was desperate to explain. "No, Chrissy, all this time I was planning to own my own place again. So I bought Oliver's farm--- not to leave you, but to stay close to you. You are the smartest, bravest, woman I have ever known. I was hoping to manage my farm and yours--- if you still need me."

"*If I still need you?*" She looked away from me and gazed at the window, where dust motes spun slowly in a sunray.

I sat in stunned silence, watching her trying hard not to cry. Was this the same woman, so strong and sure of herself, that she needed no one? As I watched, I gradually realized something I had never known, something astounding--- she really wanted *me*. It didn't matter whether I owned a farm, or not. Impossible as it seemed, I made her happy. So I slid down beside her and put my arm around her.

For the longest time, she said nothing. But then she touched my face with her warm fingers.

"I'm really happy for you, Rush. Now you have a beautiful farm of your own and the perfect place for a new rose garden."

"*We* already have a rose garden," I said.

"What about Charlie, are you taking him away?" she asked.

I started laughing. "Well, he thinks he has two homes already, so I guess he'll continue to run from one place to the other, until we decide which house is *our* home."

Chrissy took some time to digest my remark, but eventually she smiled and gently kissed my cheek, "Yes, poor Charlie. Maybe we can solve Charlie's problem right now."

## What the Wind Blew In

It was raining hard and the wind was really picking up, so I turned on my headlights and windshield wipers. My car radio was warning about a hurricane called Hugo, but hurricanes never made it this far inland, so I wasn't the least bit concerned. Heck, we had a basketball team with a mascot named Hugo, who was a harmless little hornet. I figured this Hugo might bring a lot of rain, but no big deal. Still, I needed to check on the cabin, which was a perfect excuse to get away from the hospital and the gossip.

The gossip was about Charles--- let me be more specific--- *Doctor* Charles Allen, a well-known, well- respected surgeon, who was no longer practicing at the hospital.

I met Charles right after school, when I got my first job at the Rowan Hospital. He came on to me right away, and because he was tall, dark, and handsome, I fell hook, line and sinker.

We were married two years ago, but never had time to have children. I worked in the recovery room, so after Charles performed surgery, the patients were brought to me. I thought we were happy. Money was no problem. We had a nice house on Country Club Drive, and being a member of the club was important for a surgeon. Hob knobbing with the rich and famous was how Charles built his reputation. For anybody needing surgery, Dr. Allen was the go-to guy.

Hob knobbing wasn't my cup of tea, but I pretty much had to go along. When we came home from work at night, we either went to the Club for drinks and dinner, or ate a nice hot meal the maid had prepared. Our house sat on a hill overlooking the city park. We could look out our dining room window and watch the ducks swimming around the lake. Sometimes Charles would say, "I wonder what the poor people are doing tonight?"

I loved my job. Taking care of people, even the people Charles made fun of, kept me busy and happy. But listening to the uppity old moneyed snobs at the Club bragging about their trips abroad and how their kids were doing in their Ivy League schools made me crazy.

We also had a vacation cabin located in a beautiful wooded area overlooking the Yadkin River. Charles built it as a retreat, a place to escape the stress from the hospital. He loved to fish, read, and just relax on his afternoons off.

Charles' best friend was Dr. Harvey Henderson, president of the local Medical Association. Charles and Harvey played golf every Saturday. Harvey had two children by his first wife, whom he had left to marry Ellen, his trophy bride.

The country club sponsored two fashion shows each year, and Ellen always modeled – sashaying her drop- dead figure down the runway in some gorgeous outfit provided by one of the downtown stores. Her picture was in the society pages more times than you could count.

Maybe I was a bit jealous, because I spent most of my time in a nurse's uniform giving pain medication and wiping up stuff you don't even want to know about. My patients' ailments ranged from minor surgery to bullet wounds and stabbings. Some had been cut out of car wrecks. In other words, I had seen it all.

I may not have worked out at the gym, or had my hair done by Andre and my nails done by Suzanne, but to tell the truth, I didn't really need all that artificial stuff. I had naturally curly auburn hair and blue eyes, and I kept fit by being on my feet all day. At home, I looked damn good in a pair of tight jeans.

One Saturday afternoon, when I was expecting Charles to play golf with Harvey, he informed me that he would never be playing with Harvey again.

"Because...?" I was incredulous.

"Because, I am going away."

"What on earth are you talking about?"

"I have to leave town. I can't work at the hospital anymore. I've turned all my patients over to my partner."

My body was shaking. I was in shock. I knew a *bomb* was about to drop. "Oh no, Charles, are you being sued? You have insurance for that. Honey, you are the best surgeon in town. It'll all work out. Believe me, sweetheart, everything will be all right."

"No, it won't be alright. I've been having an affair with Ellen Henderson."

I froze. My brain went dead. I sat and stared out the window at the ducks swimming peacefully around the lake, while my world fell apart.

"How long has this been going on?" I gasped.

"About a year."

"Where? Did you bring her here to our house?"

"Yes, and sometimes we went to the cabin on Wednesday afternoons when I was off. And she's pregnant."

"Well, it must be Harvey's baby." I was in complete denial.

"No, Harvey had a vasectomy, so the baby is mine. Harvey has made certain I will never work at the hospital again. Ellen left last week and rented an apartment in another town, and I'm leaving tonight to be with her. My attorney will be in touch, and I'll send a truck for my things. You can do whatever you want with what I left in the cabin."

\*\*\*

Now, as I pulled up to the cabin, still hurt and angry after all those weeks, I climbed from the car and moved some limbs that had fallen across the driveway. The river was rough, sloshing against the banks and making the pier sway back and forth.

The first things I saw when I walked inside were Charles' jacket and cap hanging on a hook beside the door. A jar of tobacco and several pipes were on the table next to his chair, and medical journals were stacked on the coffee table. The sight of all his personal things made me feel like throwing up.

I carried in a bag of groceries and put them away before getting some plastic bags to fill with the SOB's stuff. Every time I threw something in, I said a four letter word--- some were directed at Charles, but most were aimed at his bitch. I would have taken the stuff outside and set it on fire, if it hadn't been raining. In fact, I was mad enough to set the whole damn place on fire.

I wandered around the house thinking – *Did they make love on our bed, or on the sofa? Did the bitch sit at my place at the table and eat off my dishes?* The whole cabin seemed contaminated and dirty, and I felt used up and thrown away.

At 6PM I turned on the news. The weathermen were advising people to tie down porch furniture or anything that could blow away. I thought this was a waste of time, but I pulled some chairs and hanging baskets inside, and then walked down to the pier to see what needed to be done there. Sure enough, the river was rising, and Charles' little fishing boat was being tossed back and forth by the rough water.

I took a frozen dinner from the freezer, opened a bottle of wine, curled up on the sofa with a mystery, and read until I fell asleep.

Eventually, the wind howling outside and limbs falling against the house awakened me.

Suddenly I was frightened. Hugo was turning into much more than I had expected. When I opened the door to check on damage, a strange man was standing there!

I screamed in terror and tried to close the door, but the wind swept him inside, where he collapsed at my feet. He was soaked from head to toe, and the right side of his shirt was covered with blood.

"Please help me!" he moaned.

Charles kept enough medical supplies in the closet for a triage, so I grabbed a pair of scissors and cut away the stranger's shirt. He had a bullet wound in his right shoulder and was swimming and in and out of consciousness. I filled a syringe with pain medication and injected it into his arm.

*Good God, what had this man done? More importantly, what had I gotten myself into?*

But I automatically cleaned and sterilized the area around his shoulder, then boiled some forceps, which I inserted into the wound until I found the bullet and slowly pulled it out. I bandaged his shoulder and wrapped gauze around his chest, to immobilize his right arm. Infection was a real concern, until he could be seen by a doctor and given an antibiotic. Someone must have wanted him dead, but if he was on the run, he wouldn't go near a doctor.

He was surely a prison escapee. There was a prison across the river in Lexington. If he was a killer, or a bank robber, the cops were probably looking for him.

I managed to get him awake enough to move to the sofa, where I pulled off all his wet clothes, dried him with a towel, and covered him with a quilt. I took his wallet from his back pocket and checked his driver' license: Luke E. Carter, 112 East Seventh Street, Charlotte, NC.

Charles kept a pistol in the night stand by our bed, so I sat on a chair across from the sofa with the pistol in my hand. I had no phone, thanks to the storm, so I couldn't call the police. I'm not sure they could have made it from Salisbury all the way out here, anyway.

Without a doubt, Hugo was proving to be more than a hornet sting. Rain beat down on top of the cabin, trees fell and crashed all around. Suddenly the lights went out, and I lit some candles.

The man began to stir and opened his eyes. "Who are you?" I demanded.

"Luke," he gasped.

"Who shot you?'

"I don't know."

"What are you running from?'

But the man just moaned and passed out again.

Suddenly there was a loud crash, and I realized a tree had fallen across the porch. Okay, the situation had gotten way beyond scary. I was alone with a strange man that somebody had tried to kill. The killers might track him to my door. Anybody who would shoot someone in the first place wouldn't let a little wind and rain stop them from finishing the job. I didn't dare move, so I just sat with the gun pointed in his direction.

He groaned and moved restlessly for several hours, then opened his eyes and said, "I have to use the bathroom."

I leaned over and told him to put his left arm around my neck, so I could hold him and help him up.

"Why did you take all my clothes off?" He tried desperately to cover himself with the quilt.

"Because they were wet. It doesn't matter, do what I tell you, I'm a nurse. You've got nothing I haven't seen before."'

"Wait...I feel weak, like I'm going to pass out..."

"You very well might pass out. You've lost a lot of blood."

But somehow we made it to the bathroom. I stood behind him, holding him around the waist until he finished, and then I helped him back to the sofa.

He looked at his bandaged shoulder. "You got the bullet out?"

"Yes. It's over there on the coffee table, a little souvenir to take home with you. Now tell me...who shot you?"

"I told you, I really don't know."

"What are you running from?"

"I'm not running..." he said as he drifted off again.

I listened to weather reports on my transistor radio with my gun pointed at him until dawn. The storm was still raging outside. I looked out the window at the devastation Hugo had caused. A lawn chair was upside down in the walkway, and a pump cover lay at the foot of my steps. My patient was still asleep.

I needed a caffeine fix in the worst way, and something to eat. I lit the gas grill on the back porch, managed to make coffee, and then took my cup back to the den.

Luke, or whoever he was, opened his eyes. He sat up, looked around the room, and then glanced out the window at the storm damage. "Did you point that gun at me all night?"

"Yes, who are you running from?"

"*I'm* not running from anyone. Who are *you* running from? I'll bet you're running from something. Why are you down here all by yourself? Don't you have a husband?"

"I do, and he'll be here to check on me soon."

"No, he won't. He can't get here. It'll be days before all the downed trees are removed, and you'll be one of the last to get your power back. Believe me, I know. You and I are prisoners here."

"Did you escape from prison?" I asked.

"I am not a criminal," he insisted. "And I don't feel like arguing. Can you give me something for pain?"

I took him a cup of coffee and a pain pill. "Now I'm going to make us some breakfast on the grill. You need to eat, if you want to heal." He smiled. "Don't forget your gun."

I helped him sit up and put a pillow behind his back. His right arm was still bound to his body and he was too groggy to use his left, so I sat on the coffee table and fed him some toast and eggs.

"Why do you care if I heal? If you're so afraid of me, why didn't you let me die?"

"I'm a nurse, and I took an oath."

Later, I changed his bandage. The wound didn't look good, and I was concerned about infection. I heated some water, bathed his chest and swabbed the wound with disinfectant. I got one of Charles' shirts, some underwear, and pair of pants and told him to get dressed. But he passed out before I finished my sentence.

When I realized he was probably going to sleep most of the day, I lay down on my bed.

It was about 5PM when I woke up. He still hadn't dressed, was still wrapped in the quilt, reading my mystery.

"Pretty scary book! Were you reading this last night, *Murder in the Moonlight?* My god, the woman in the novel gets dragged into the woods, raped and murdered. Then after reading all that, I showed up at your door. No wonder you were scared, Louisa. "

"How do you know my name?"

"It's written inside your book. It says: *To Louisa, Happy Birthday, from Charles.*"

I pointed the gun at him. "Put on some clothes before I put a bullet in your other shoulder."

"You've got my right arm bandaged to my chest. How am I supposed to get dressed? Heck, I'm getting used to lying around naked.

I kinda like it, and besides, I'm only half way through *Murder in the Moonlight*. Did you ever find out who did it, Louisa?"

I had been so stressed since Charles' *bomb* dropped, and now I had to deal with this smart ass man lying on my sofa reading my book. It was beginning to dawn on me that I really *was* a prisoner. This could go on for days, and I simply couldn't cope much longer. I was emotionally exhausted. I was losing control, and I started to cry.

"What are you running from Louisa? Your husband? All those bags are filled with Charles' things. Where is he? "Luke asked softly.

"I don't know where the hell he is, and he's not my husband anymore. And you're right, he won't be coming here anytime soon, so you might as well kill or rape me, if that's your plan. I'm too tired to care."

He laughed and shook his head. "Was it another woman?"

"Yes, damn it!" I sobbed. "He had an affair with his best friend's wife, and now she's going to have his baby."

"Keep talking, I'm a good listener."

"God, I need a drink. My piece of shit husband collects imported wines and chocolates, and I am going to open the most expensive bottle I can find," I said as I stomped to the kitchen.

I returned with a bottle of red wine from Papel Valley, Chile, and when I handed him a glass, he said, "You're exhausted, Louisa. Come sit beside me and relax. Tell me everything that happened..."

Something about his gentle manner allowed me to confide. "Charles dumped me for the most gorgeous woman in town, and he got her pregnant. I'm sure they'll have a beautiful baby. Everybody at the hospital is whispering behind my back, and it's the juiciest gossip at the Club, not that I'm ever going *there* again. They probably had sex in our bed, and right here on this sofa where we are sitting."

He let me talk for a long time before he handed me another glass of wine. "Louisa, it's not your fault. Charles cheated on you. People aren't talking about you, they are blaming him. You are strong. You will recover, I promise."

For the first time in weeks, I felt less sorry for myself. I looked curiously at the man seated beside me. "What about you, Luke? Do you have a wife?"

He thought carefully before he answered. "I have an ex-wife, and she has remarried. We dated a few times in high school, ended up in the back seat of my car, and you can figure out the rest. We have a daughter, so we tried to make it work. But in the end, we just weren't right together, so we decided not to be unhappy the rest of our lives."

Later that evening, I cooked some noodles on the grill, opened a jar of spaghetti sauce, and carried the food to the coffee table. We ate by candlelight, finished the bottle of red wine and I opened a box of Ademei Porcelana chocolates from Venezuela.

The sun was shining when I woke up the next morning. I lit the grill again, and then made coffee and some breakfast. Eventually, I walked outside. Trees were down everywhere, and the ones left standing were stripped of their leaves. An old maple had crashed through my windshield. It was obvious we weren't going anywhere for a very long time.

"Will someone come looking for you?" he asked.

"No, nobody knows where I am. How about you?"

"Yes, I expect Duke Power will be looking for my body there in the river. But right now, their first priority is restoring power to our customers."

"You work for Duke Power?"

"Yes, I'm an engineer. I came to the Buck Steam Plant here on the Yadkin to check the water levels for a possible breach in the lower dam. We were doing everything we could to prepare for a possible hit from the hurricane. "I was in a boat inspecting the dam when it got so rough I could hardly keep the boat upright. I radioed the station saying I was going to head in, and that's when I felt the jolt that almost knocked me overboard. When I saw blood oozing from my shirt I became dizzy and sick on my stomach. All I could think about was my daughter and how I didn't want her to grow up without a father. Then I felt the river swallowing me. The last thing I remember was pulling my head out of the water and coughing to clear my lungs."

"But who would shoot you?"

"I don't know, a stray bullet from a hunter is my guess. I don't remember much after that, except the pain. Anyway, I washed up on your doorstep. If you hadn't been here, I would have bled to death. I could never have survived this storm."

He paused to shift into a more comfortable position. "And I have to tell you, Louisa, you weren't the only one who was scared. The pain medication made me hallucinate. Every time I opened my eyes, I was staring down the barrel of your gun. In the beginning, I thought *you* shot me, and when you bandaged my arm to my chest, I thought you were tying my hands. I wanted to escape, but you had taken my clothes to keep me from running. It was really a horrible nightmare."

By the time Luke finished describing his vision of me as a murderer, we were both laughing about the crazy circumstances we found ourselves in.

"Luke, you take the bed tonight, I'll sleep on the sofa. You need a good night's sleep." "Only if you sleep beside me," he said.

We made do as best as we could. We read John Grisham and Steven King mysteries, listened to music on the transistor radio and played card games. One evening I built a bonfire in the back yard and burned all of Charles' things--- except the books, which Luke begged me save.

I cooked thawed meat on the grill and pretty much cleaned out the pantry except for some canned beans.

"Looks like it will be black beans and bread tonight," I said. A bottle of Sangiovese from Tuscany should go well with that and we'll have Pierre Marcolini chocolates from Brussels for desert."

Luke's wound was healing nicely. The risk of infection seemed unlikely, so I was able to cover it with a smaller bandage. I heated water on the grill for each of us to have a warm bath. Luke shaved with Charles' razor, but I threatened to lock him out of the cabin if he came out of the bathroom wearing Charles' cologne.

Finally, we had to get serious about being rescued. We were running out of food, the wine was gone, and we both realized it was time to face reality. On the fourth night of our ordeal, we decided we should walk out to the highway the next morning, flag down a car, and ask for help.

Luke said, "Louisa, do you really want to go home?"

I sighed. "No, I dread entering the house I once shared with Charles, and I hate the idea of going back to the hospital, but damn, I'm hungry."

"People will have forgotten about the scandal, Louisa. The only thing they'll be talking about is the day Hugo hit. What are you going to say when they ask you how you weathered the storm?"

"I'll tell them I was trapped in a secluded cabin down by the Yadkin River, where the wind blew like crazy and trees crashed all around me. Then I'll tell them I opened the door, and *you'll never believe what the wind blew in*--- a handsome stranger with blonde hair and a bullet in his shoulder.

He could have died, but he wanted to live and be happy. So did I. What will you tell them, Luke?"

"I'll say that I got shot in the shoulder, almost drowned in the river, washed up on the doorstep of a woman who drugged me, took my clothes off, tied my hands, held me at gunpoint, raped me, and made me *real* happy."

"I don't seem to remember that last part, Luke. You know--- that part about me raping you...? Wish I'd thought of it."      "It's not too late." He grinned.

# There Are Books Left to Write

We had picked out names for either a boy, or a girl. Our boy lived for about an hour---long enough for Teri and me to hold him and say goodbye.

Afterwards, Dr. Monroe explained, in his medical, matter-of-fact way, that we had the RH negative blood factor. "Every pregnancy is different. The next one could be perfectly normal," he said.

It was a while before Teri went back to her job, teaching third grade at the local elementary school. I taught in the English department at Davidson College.

Davidson is a quiet little college town with tree lined streets, several churches and a nice library overlooking the village green--- the perfect place to raise a family. We bought a brick house with enough bedrooms to accommodate the large family we had planned. It was located not far from the college and close enough for our children to walk to school.

Our backyard was shaded by big oak trees, filled with Teri's flowers, my bird feeders, a brick barbeque, and a picnic table. The previous owners, who had children, had added a fence and a child's swing set. Every time we looked out the kitchen window, we saw the empty swings – waiting to be filled.

After doing some research on the RH negative blood factor, I learned that it didn't ruin every pregnancy, and Teri's doctor encouraged her to try again.

This time everything seemed fine until near the end of the eighth month, when Teri couldn't feel the baby moving. Our greatest fears were confirmed--- no heartbeat. Dr. Monroe scheduled a cesarean section, and for the second time, we said good-bye to a beautiful baby boy.

Those who have never lost a baby cannot imagine the sadness one experiences. I worried about my wife and her mental state until we found a grief counselor, and with her help, we decided to adopt.

Teri's grandparents had emigrated from Northern Italy, so we traveled to the village where they had lived, hoping to adopt an Italian child. After several years of legal setbacks and disappointments, we gave up.

Years later, Teri was diagnosed with breast cancer. She was a real trooper dealing with her chemo and radiation. For two years, she fought as hard as she could, until her body could take no more.

***

One warm September afternoon, the new school year was about to begin when I walked across the street to the local bookstore. I passed the bank on the corner and several shops displaying *Welcome Back Students* signs written in red and black, the school colors.

I was about to enter the store, when I stopped to look at a book displayed in the window. On the cover was a picture of a sandy beach under a blue sky, and in the background, an old weather- beaten cottage surrounded by sea oats. The title was: *Low Country Secrets,* by Meredith Sinclair.

Shock waves ran through my body as I read the sign beside it: Davidson College graduate here for book signing--- September 15, 5:00 – 6:00 PM.

165

\*\*\*

It was during my first year teaching at the college, my very first creative writing class that she walked in and took a seat on the front row. Her long black hair fell across smooth tanned shoulders--- probably from spring break at the beach. She was wearing plaid shorts, and I watched as she placed her shapely brown legs under the desk, opened her notebook, and raised her beautiful, dark brown eyes to meet mine.

I was twenty- seven, and she was twenty- two. Something happened between us that simply could not be explained. It was a kind of magnetism--- a meeting of the souls, or maybe just a hormone rush. I couldn't explain it, but it happened.

She stayed after class one day to ask what I would suggest she do to improve an essay I had assigned. Knowing damn well that wasn't the real reason she stayed, I pulled up a chair so close our legs brushed, and it was no accident when my hand touched hers as we made changes in her work.

That's how it began. Our love affair continued in my apartment for the rest of the semester. It was exciting and sexual. I found it incredibly hard to teach my class, while remembering how I had kissed her nude body and slept with her curled around me the night before.

She wanted to be a writer, and I certainly encouraged her, but she wasn't the best student in my class. She knew I couldn't be impartial when critiquing her assignments, so eventually she stopped telling me what she was working on.

She teased me mercilessly about those lectures in which I said, "A writer is the sum total of his or her life experiences, so think of yourself as a sponge."

Sometimes before we made love, she laughed and said "I'm a sponge, Matt, waiting for a life experience."

She played my Van Morrison album endlessly: *"Have I told you lately that I love you? Have I told you there is no one else above you? Fill my heart with gladness, take away my sadness, ease my troubles, that's what you do."*

On the last day of classes, she was still in bed when I left to teach. She had stayed up late the night before, working on her final assignment, and it was 9:02 when she rushed late in into the class room.

Her hair was still damp from the shower, and it smelled of my shampoo. Neither of us made eye contact, pretending she was just another student, but my throbbing body knew better.

A week later, I was in my office putting on my cap and gown, to march with the faculty into the auditorium for graduation, when the phone rang:

"Matt, this is Dad. I found your mother unconscious. She isn't breathing, and I can't find a pulse. I've called 911. I need you to come home."

I never saw Meredith again

\*\*\*

I bought a book, even though I'd already read it, and turned to the back page, where I found her picture. Her beautiful black hair, now streaked with silver, was pulled back into a pony tail. And her brown eyes seemed to be looking right into mine, bringing back all the old sensations that had been buried deep within me.

Underneath the picture I read: *Meredith Sinclair is a graduate of Davidson College, Davidson, North Carolina and The University of South Carolina, where she earned her Master's Degree. She lives in Charleston, South Carolina. She has one daughter, three grandchildren, and a dog named Rosie.*

I held her book cradled in my arms as I stood in line waiting to have it signed. My stomach did flip flops--- a combination of terror and ecstasy as I approached her.

She raised her enchanting eyes and said, "Matt! I was hoping I might see you, but I didn't know if you were still teaching here. How should sign your book?"

"Surprise me." I managed a shy smile. "I'd like to wait around until you have finished, and then we can go to the Soda Shop--- unless you have other plans."

She had no other plans.

We each ordered a sandwich and coffee.

"This sure brings back good memories," she said. "Remember when we used to come here? By the way, how did you like my book? You did read it, didn't you?"

"It's a great book. I loved your description of the old cottage and the way you handled the mystery, keeping the reader in suspense until the very last page. You set it up perfectly for a sequel.

"I've missed you, Meredith."

She gave me an odd, searching look.

"What happened, Matt? After graduation, I rushed to your office to see you before I left for home, but you weren't there. Your gown was thrown over your chair, so I went to your apartment, but it was locked. A neighbor said she'd seen you put a suitcase in the car and leave...

"You didn't say goodbye, Matt. I sat on your steps and cried – thinking that you loved me, when in truth, I meant nothing to you."

"My god, Meredith, I loved you more than anything! While I was getting ready for graduation, my father called and told me that my mother was gravely ill. I left town immediately.

"I called your house right after the funeral, but your mother said you were not available. I explained that I needed to talk to you, and asked her to have you call me. When you didn't, I thought you didn't want *me*. I was afraid you had someone else. Did you ever marry?"

"Yes, for a brief time. It only lasted two years, and you?"

"My wife, Teri died last year. Meredith, please come home with me, there are things we need to talk about."

"Yes," she said, "There are some things."

We soon found that the mutual attraction and passion still sparked between us. We were like two lost souls that had been rejoined.

"Do you have children?" she asked.

"No, unfortunately, I don't."

Then, she seemed to choke on her own words, "Yes, you do, Matt.

"What?"

170

In a voice that was little more than a whisper, she said, "You have a daughter."

"I don't understand."

"Matt, two months after I left school, I learned I was pregnant. Your daughter's name is Megan McDonald, and you are the father listed on her birth certificate. That's the real reason I'm here. She wants to meet you.

"I didn't know if you were married, or how you would feel about her, but I promised Megan I would try to arrange a meeting."

Meredith pulled a photo from her wallet and handed it to me. "This is your daughter," she said.

I was crying when Meredith put her arms around me.

"She really wants to meet you. She'll be here tomorrow, if you say *yes*."

"Yes!" I sobbed.

"She will also be bringing your three grandchildren."

"My three *grandchildren*?" I stammered.

"Yes, you're a grandfather, and your family really wants to meet you, Matt."
"Oh, my god! My family?"

She kissed me and said, "Well, yeah, the one we started one night in your apartment. You know how you preached in class, "Soak up life like an empty sponge? Well, I did."

My family arrived the next afternoon. My heart was pounding, and I couldn't hold back the tears when my daughter approached, put her arms around me, and said:

"Hello Dad!"

Life experiences were coming at me so fast and so furiously, it felt like being in a three ring circus. And I was expected to be in all three rings at the same time. I had a two year old boy crawling in my lap saying, "Read Grandpa," and two little girls following me around the house competing for my attention and asking one question after another.

Soon it seemed like being a father and grandfather was the most natural thing in the world, and I cherished every minute of it.

These days my wife, the novelist, is writing another book - the sequel to *Low Country Secrets.* Occasionally, she will accept criticism from her former professor, which seems only fair to me, since she named the villain *Matt.*

I am writing a book too - a romance novel based on my life's experiences with, *You Know Who* and now *she* critiques me. Her latest comment: "My god, Matt, this borders on porn."

You be the judge--- it will be out soon in a store near you.

# A Time and a Place

My roommate shook me and screamed, "Richard, the building is on fire!"

It wasn't yet daylight and I couldn't see my hand in front of my face. Screams were coming from all over the third floor. Boys were rushing like crazy to get down the steps. Some of us tried to put the fire out before we realized it was hopeless. Thick black smoke was choking me and making my eyes burn as I threw my sheets, blanket and some clothes out the window.

I grabbed my violin and went to stand outside in the freezing November weather to watch the Chambers building burn to the ground.

The sun was just coming up when Davidson College President, Dr. William Martin, gathered us refuges around the well. We would all be temporarily placed in the homes of professors or town's people.

Miss Sally, who lived in a big white frame house on Main Street, welcomed me into her home and treated me like royalty. I wasted no time writing my mother to let her know of our misfortune and that I was without most basic needs and totally without funds.

The other boys moved back on campus as soon as they could, but I decided to stay on with Miss Sally. She was the youngest of eight children, never married, and took in borders to make ends meet. She let me eat free for a while, in exchange for me doing odd jobs around the house. Her good food was reason enough to stay, and her place already felt like home.

My mother, Anna Cowan, lived on a sheep farm in the mountains of Virginia. David, my brother, had been taking care of the farm since my father's death. My family was disappointed that I too had not become a sheep farmer, but I was so unlike my brother. I wasn't really built for that kind of hard work, and not at all interested.

From as far back as I could remember, I was drawn to music. My heart jumped for joy when I heard my neighbors gather and play mountain songs. I had asked for a fiddle for Christmas one year, and I will never forget coming downstairs and finding my very own fiddle under the tree. I can't explain it, but I knew how to play the minute I placed it under my chin and drew the bow across the strings.

In my freshman year I joined the college orchestra and loved it when we all played our various instruments--- coming together to make beautiful music. That year I also discovered my love of history and made it my major.

I was a senior when Mother came down with cancer. Well, at least that was when I first learned about it. When I went home for Christmas, I saw how sick she was. My days on the farm that December made me realize I would never live there again.

I graduated in May of 1925. Our class gift to the school was to replace the old wooden well with a new brick structure designed by the architect of the new Chambers Building. We had a saying around campus concerning that well:

*It's queer the many things they tell about our dear old college well; no aged man could ever glean the knowledge of things it has seen.*

The college offered me an Assistant Professorship in the History Department, and Davidson was destined to become my home forever.

176

Right after graduation, I went back to the farm and took care of Mother until she died in July. She was buried at the little Baptist church on the side of a mountain beside my father. She expected her children to be buried there as well, so she could spend eternity beside them.

After the funeral, I went through Mother's belongings, hoping to distribute them as she would have wanted. In one special drawer, I found photos of us as kids, a photo of Mother's first Thanksgiving with all the Cowan cousins, one of me and my dog
Sammy, plus cards and newspaper clippings. Two of these clippings were yellowed with age.

The two articles were from *The Statesboro, NC Record and Landmark,* dated September, 1903. The first headline was *Mount Villa Man Murdered*:

"Randall Sherwell was shot in the early morning hours at his home in Mount Villa by the Black brothers from a neighboring county. The brothers claimed Sherwell had ruined their niece. They gave Mr. Sherwell a choice: either he could go with them and marry their niece--- or be shot. When Mr. Sherwell refused to accompany them, he received two gun shots to the head."

The second article covered the trial of the Black brothers and the testimony of Mr. Sherwell's mother, Sarah, who described the shooting and the death of her son. The Black brother's "ruined" niece, Anna, who has since married and moved to Virginia, was expected to testify but was unable to attend because of the illness of her baby. The Black brothers were sentenced to six years in prison.

That day I sat on Mother's bed with the newspaper articles spread across my lap for a long time, my mind in utter confusion. Was this Anna Black possibly *my* mother? My first memories – what were they? Mostly of this old house, the room upstairs that I shared with David, the horse Daddy gave me when I was thirteen, my dog Sammy, and helping with the sheep.

But there had to be a reason Mother kept these articles hidden away. Surely David Cowan, the man who raised me, was my natural father. He just was. He had loved me unconditionally, and he had been the best father any boy could ask for...

Yet, my mother had never really discussed her family. All she ever told me was that she was an orphan, raised by a woman named Lessie.

I didn't really want to know any more about this Anna Black from North Carolina, or the Sherwells. I didn't even want to think about those people or that ugly story. I wanted it to stay in the past.

So I gathered Mother's clothes and took them to a church in Danville that collected things for the needy. When I passed the court house, though, the historian in me took over and pulled into a parking space in front of the building. I walked up the steps and right into the Register of Deeds office. It was there I found the evidence I sought – David Richard Cowan married Anna Mae Black on November 1, 1903, at Sandy Creek Baptist Church.

My birth certificate read "James Richard Cowan, born to David Richard Cowan and Anna Mae Cowan on February 15, 1904."

I had been born only three and a half months after my parents married!

The proof was right before my eyes. I was not who I thought I was. In fact, I was likely the son of the murdered Randall Sherwell, so somewhere I might have another family. I would never be a whole person until I knew the rest of my history. And as painful as that might be, I knew I had to find out.

\*\*\*

I had no idea where Mount Villa was, but learned it was only twenty miles from Davidson College.

It proved to be a lovely little country village with a depot, post office, flour mill and a general store with a sign out front that read *Sherwell's Store.*

I parked my car near the air pump outside the building, walked under a covered walkway up the steps, and opened a screen door covered with peeling green paint.

One side of the store displayed overalls, shirts, work boots, and socks. On the other side were shelves of canned goods and a candy counter. In the back, I saw a meat counter and an office. Two big fans were oscillating at full speed, trying to relieve the Southern August heat. I pulled an ice cold Coca Cola from the drink box and bought a package of cheese crackers.

It felt so strange. Who were these people? Should I recognize them? Who were they to me? And would they even care who I was, or why I was here?

"Do you know Sarah Sherwell?" I shyly asked the clerk.

"Well, of course, I do. Sarah owns this store. She lives right yonder in that house you see under them big oak trees."

"Do you know where the Sherwells are buried?" I asked.

"Yes, that'd be down at Shady Creek Church, and it's just about two miles on down this road."

When I reached the church, I walked across the newly mowed lawn to the cemetery. It was so quiet. Only a few birds sang in the stately pine trees that stood in respectful attention over a field of granite headstones.

I quickly found Adam Sherwell's grave. At the foot was a brass cross that indicated he had fought in the Civil War. To one side was a smaller stone that read: Randall Sherwell, born April 1882, died September 1903.

Tears came to my eyes as I stood looking at the moss covered stone. Silently I wondered why Randall would rather die at the hands of the Black brothers rather than marry my mother and acknowledge being my father. I knew I would never know the answer, and Randall would never know what he missed.

I returned to old Sarah Sherwell's house, climbed the stone steps, walked across the porch where my father lay dying, and knocked on Sarah's door. When she answered, she seemed so fragile and unsteady, I thought she might fall.

"Mrs. Sherwell," I began nervously. "My name is Richard Cowan. My mother grew up in this area, and I'd like to come in and talk to you, if I may."

She showed me in and asked me to have a seat. Her white hair, like fresh-polished silver, was wound into a knot on top of her head. Her gold- framed glasses slid down the narrow bridge of her nose.

The white shawl draped around her shoulders framed a pale lavender dress. "Please forgive me for staring..." she said as she squinted at me. "But you look so much like my son. Who are you, and what do you want?"

"My mother died recently, and I found some newspaper articles among her things that led me to you. Anna Black was my mother, and I believe your son was my father. Didn't you ever wonder      what happened to      your grandchild?"

"If you're talking about those awful Black brothers, no! I couldn't stand to think much about them. That period in my life was like a bad dream. I never knew what the Blacks did with that child, but I knew they'd never let me see it...

"Yes, it was a painful thing, knowing there was a child of Randall's out there somewhere. That child was a part of me, too. But if you have anything to do with those people, I don't think we have much to talk about."

She paused a minute to let her mind catch up, and then said, "You say you're Anna Black's son?"

I handed her the newspaper articles. She looked at them carefully, then slowly said, "Well, I guess you could be my grandson."

"Mrs. Sherwell, I checked my parent's marriage license and my birth certificate, and now I don't have one doubt in my mind. The discovery gives me no pleasure. You see, I grew up on a sheep farm with wonderful parents, and I had a happy life. But now I now know it was all a lie."

She twisted a white handkerchief in her hands, and I could see how uncomfortable she was at having to relive the past.

"I'm sorry I've upset you, and I won't keep you any longer," I said. "But I'll be teaching at Davidson College next year, and now that I know the truth, I hope you'll allow me to visit again. Perhaps you'll be so kind as to share some things about my father...?"

With these words, I was prepared to go, but Sarah reached out and touched my sleeve.

"No, wait, young man! I need to think more about what you have told me. I never expected this, you see. It all happened such a long time ago. But seeing you here today, it's almost like having my Randall home again."

She left the room for a few minutes and came back with a box of photographs. She handed me one depicting a handsome young man, a fellow a girl could fall easily fall in love with. He was tall, slender, his head held high. He had a shotgun slung across his shoulder and two bird dogs at his feet. His wavy brown hair swept across his face and fell to one side, almost covering his left eye. I felt my hand pushing my hair away from the left side of my face.

"I wish Randall had done the honorable thing and married your mother." Mrs. Sherwell sadly shook her head. "I blame myself for Randall's bad behavior. I had five girls before he was born. I spoiled him, and so did his sisters. He was "king of the roost" in a house full of girls. My husband told me I would be sorry, and he was right."

She handed me another picture of Randall on a horse, and one of him standing behind his father, who was holding a fiddle.

"My grandfather played a fiddle?" I asked incredulously.

"He had music in every bone in his body. He loved to play for anybody who would listen to him. His fiddle hasn't been played since the day he died."

A few minutes later, she placed the case in my lap. I opened it and slowly removed the old instrument, worn with use, and placed it under my chin.

"Tell me what he played for you."

"My husband used to play *In the Sweet By and By,*" she said, a faraway look in her eyes. "It was my favorite."

I drew the bow across the strings and played the song for her. When I finished, her old eyes were full of tears.

"Oh, you bring back so many memories! You could be Adam sitting there, or Randall. You look so much like them both. My Adam would want you to have his fiddle. Nobody else in the family can play it."

\*\*\*

After that day, I went back to live at Miss Sally's and began a long teaching career at Davidson College. In 1929, the new Chambers building was completed, and I moved into my new office.

I began attending the Presbyterian Church, where the prettiest girl I ever saw played the piano. I joined the choir just so I could get to know Miss Rebecca Little, who later became my wife.

When Miss Sally became too old to manage the boarding house, I bought it from her, and Rebecca and I looked after Miss Sally and the boarders.

My Sherwell relatives never did accept me as part of the family. It seemed I was an embarrassment they didn't want to acknowledge. They didn't even tell me when my grandmother Sarah died, but in the years that followed, I went to the cemetery every year and placed flowers on her grave.

I never told anybody my secret, not even Rebecca.

One day I woke up and realized I had become an old man. Some days, when I felt up to it, I walked down to the old well on campus and sat on the bench beside it.

Ivy wound up the brick columns at the well, and yellow daffodils bloomed around its base. Happy memories filled my mind. Long ago, I told the well the truth about me. The Sherwell family was our secret now---- just mine and the well's.

*No aged man could ever glean, the knowledge of things it has seen...and heard.*

## About the Author

Betsey Barber Hampton lives in Davidson, North Carolina. In her early years she was happiest in front of an easel, paint brush in hand. She was interested in anything ART and loved showing her works at Merrill-Jennings Galleries.

Now in her eighties and handicapped, Betsey enjoys writing short stories and doing genealogy.

*"These short stories are a result of recalling people and places from the past. A desire to trace my roots led to researching my ancestors back to England, Ireland, and Scotland. I have tried to imagine who they were and what their lives were like. Some of these ghosts reappeared as voices in my head telling me what to write. These stories are a tribute to them and a way of saying 'Thanks' for sending me down this path. I wish I could have known you."*